W9-BGT-977

WHEN
WE WAS
FIERCE

WHEN WE WAS FIERCE

e.E. Charlton-Trujillo

CANDLEWICK PRESS

Copyright © 2016 by e.E. Charlton-Trujillo

p. vii: Excerpt from "Only God Can Judge Me":
Words and music by Tupac Shakur, Anthony Forte, Harold Fretty,
and Douglas Rasheed. Copyright © 1996 by Universal Music Corp.;
Universal–Songs of Polygram International, Inc.; Madcastle Muzic;
Game Plan Music; Songs of Universal, Inc.; and Rag Top Publishing.
All rights for Madcastle Muzic administered by Universal–Songs
of Polygram International, Inc. All rights for Rag Top Publishing
administered by Songs of Universal, Inc. All Rights Reserved. Used
by Permission. Reprinted by Permission of Hal Leonard Corporation.
Lyrics copyright © 1996 by Game Plan Music,
used by permission of Harold Scrap Fretty.

First edition 2016

Library of Congress Catalog Card Number pending
ISBN 978-0-7636-7937-8

16 17 18 19 20 21 BVG 10 9 8 7 6 5 4 3 2 1

Printed in Berryville, VA, U.S.A.

This book was typeset in Meridien.

Candlewick Press
99 Dover Street
Somerville, Massachusetts 02144

visit us at www.candlewick.com

Gordo, your faith in this story kept the fire wild and the fierce alive. I will forever be grateful.

I'd rather die like a man than live like a coward.

Tupac Shakur

Ricky-Ricky

We wasn't up to nuthin' new, really.
Me and Jimmy, Catch and Yo-Yo.
We just comin' down the street, keepin' cool.
We was good at stayin' low.
Especially around the Wooden Spoon.
Guys hang around there, they got teeth on 'em.
Sharper than broken glass. Words that slit ya
from chin to belly. And that's *just* their words.

So.
My bad day started with this good kid Ricky-Ricky.
We called him that 'cause the fool always
repeatin' himself.
Like he might say, "I was down on the corner—
down on the corner, that's where I was."

Only, second time he say it, it
would have this stutter-confusion thing.
Like maybe he didn't get he'd been there.

Anyways, we all cut up the alley
'cross the street.
Watchin' that fool,
that whiz-wonder Ricky-Ricky,
strut up to the Wooden Spoon.

Jimmy threw a finger spin on the basketball
he'd been hooking all summer.

"I'm gonna get me some play from Gabs with
this. Check it," Jimmy say, bouncing that ball
midair, tricking.

I just laugh. He always angling to get some girl
loose from her moral. That just his way.

"That guy slap stupid," say Catch 'bout Ricky-Ricky.

"I don't even wanna watch," say Yo-Yo, spinning his
throwback bullet-red Duncan. "I don't know *what*
he thinkin'."

Ricky-Ricky was thinkin' he'd make cool with those guys.
Thinkin' they'd make cool back on account of his
older brother Big Joe rollin' outta the Pen soon.
Word 'round the block was that the sides,
Black vs. Brown,
were "under talks" about territory.

Who gets to sling where, when, and more.
And Big Joe?
He was on keepin' the peace between both.
Sorta.

But Ricky-Ricky ain't nuthin' hard like Big Joe.
Fo' sure.
He wasn't no slinger.
He too soft-skulled to come outta the rain.
Kid eat fifty-cent candy for a nickel
from the corner bodega.
Bodega guy don't charge him cost
'cause he Mighty Mildred's grandkid.
And people in the hood . . . they hold
r e s p e c t
for her.
She was an original foot soldier.
Brother King. March on D.C.
She rolled with 'em all.

"Hey, let's cut out," Jimmy say. "I ain't
got no time to be foolin'."

But that kid Ricky-Ricky had went right
up to Money Mike and Jay Ridge
standing that corner.
Held up his hand for a high five.
Them guys looked at him like he was
mad-cray times twelve,
and the four of us looked the same.

Now, we don't know what was said on

the *real*, 'cause we was hangin' so far back,
but that fool got out a few words.
Enough fo' him to think he worked those
guys good, 'cause he was smiling.
That kid had a way to glow.

Then—

BAM!

Money Mike slammed Ricky-Ricky across the jaw.
That kid busted open like a piñata.
Only something sweet supposed to come outta
a piñata.
Wasn't nothing sweet comin' outta Ricky-Ricky.

Us guys, we leaned back like we was some
choreographed boy band.
All at once we say, *"Damn . . . ,"* and winced.

Jay Ridge and a couple other guys jumped in.
Fists and feet full-flying, but Money Mike tore
through them, raging.
He was intent.
And that kid Ricky-Ricky cried out!

People peeped out curtains—tipped their heads out
their doors.
But ain't nobody step.
Ain't nobody's cool.
Especially with Money Mike
stomp-breaking that kid to pieces.

When them guys peeled back, Ricky-Ricky shriveled
and shrunk.
I could barely see he was a boy
way he was all rolled up
on the heat of the concrete.
He look like that pile a clothes my sister, Monica, threw
out the window when she caught Buffalo cheating.

Catch chuckled. "Shit! That's one *flat* fool!"

"*Shh* . . ." say Yo-Yo. "Don't invite."

"Don't *shh* me, fool," say Catch.

Yo-Yo whipped that Duncan into his palm and
held it tight.

"You wanna borrow attention?" ask Jimmy.
"'Cause it don't look like they playin'."

"Whatever. Shit . . ." Catch looked to me. "Man, T . . .
you'd think *every* punk ten blocks out be schooled
after they see your whooping."

I stuck my chest out, shoulders back.
"That joke ain't timeless, Catch," I say.

I drew my hands into a fist.

"You got something fo' me?" I ask.

Jimmy stepped between us.

He could see we was heated.
Real heated.

Catch laughed. "That's how it is?"

He danced and bobbed around Jimmy
like he was ringing up
at Luther's Gym.
Broken beer bottles cracking
under his fast new sneaks.
They were hotter than the watch on his
stepdaddy's wrist.

"T's got school in session for Catch," he say.

He on big with his grin.
Savoring up on my flavor of pissed.

I didn't blink, even if my lids were shakin'.
"Don't test it," I say.

Jimmy pushed his arms out to keep us distant.
"Come on, guys," say Jimmy. "Why we wanna
work up like this? We're even. We're even, right?
C'mon. Let's make for the Court."

Catch cut me good with his stare.
It was lined with his mama's slaps and his
stepdaddy's belt buckle.
Catch played hard better than me and knew it.
It burned me up something deep.

"Don't play me fool, Catch," I say. "I'll bust you
up and break you down."

"Oh, yeah?" ask Catch.

He shot out two easy jabs.
It didn't excite me forward.
I was too heated to be drawn out with play jabs.

"Enough, yo," say Jimmy.

But Jimmy done been a fool
and stepped straight between us
just as Catch pump-jabbed.

BAM!

Jimmy took it across the jaw.
That throw connect hard.

"Shit, beast!" Jimmy was raw at Catch!
"What the fuck, Negro?"

"Don't talk slaves to me.
Stay out between this, smalls," warned Catch.

"Beat it down, then," say Jimmy. "Not my cool."

We kept our loose dance in rotation.

"Well?" ask Catch.

"You gonna lay off me?" I ask him. "You
been poking a stick all day."

Catch fake-pumped a punch, then
hooked me at the neck, knuckling my head.

"Man, you had me goin', T," say Catch.
He was laughing his ass wild.

"You gettin' hard, man. You all
'That joke ain't timeless.' That speak got
flavor."

I wasn't holding humor fo' him.
He been poking it at me all week
one way to the other.

"I ain't playin'," I say, workin' to get him
to turn me loose.

He just laugh as the hook 'round my
neck spun us.
We was twisting wild
when Yo-Yo sounded off in one of 'em
loud Yo-Yo whispers, "Hey, guys. Guys!
Ricky-Ricky still ain't movin'. He look flat-fixed
on the real maybe."

I shove Catch off, and he lose his step a bit.

"You really heated at me?" Catch ask.

I held my chin hard.
Hard as I could do given my lack of tough.

"A'ight . . ." Catch put up hands. "I'm cool."

Jimmy had his nose around the corner.
Yo-Yo right beside him.
Catch cut up next Jimmy.

"What you mean he ain't movin'?" ask Catch.

And then I stepped right in and seen it too.

Ricky-Ricky was straight still as could be.
Money Mike and Jay Ridge were nowhere in sight.
That fool kid had done got himself beat flat.
Flatter than when Money Mike whooped me,
and that was saying something.

"We can't leave him there," say Yo-Yo.

"What's this *we* shit?" Catch ask. "That fool
walk *right up* there himself. He know not to go near
the Wooden 'less he wants a whoopin'. Damn,
you more fool than fat. And that's a lot given that
fudge-pudge belly."

Catch kept smiling. It was the kind of smile
that burned Yo-Yo straight up and down.
They weren't good as stepbrothers.
Not good at all.

Jimmy whipped mad spin on the basketball.
"Let's get out. I got hoop to shoot and girls to
dazzle. Somebody come up in a few."

The guys peeled off the wall and headed down
the alley.
But me.
Me,
I waited.
Waited to see if Ricky-Ricky would get up.
If some part of him, a leg—an arm—something—
would move.
Waited for some kind of proof that he wasn't plucked.
But nothing.

"T!" Jimmy call out.

"Yo-Yo's right," I say. "Can't leave him there. Not like that."

"Somebody help," say Catch, all gruff. "Hell,
Old Man Charlie will pull Ricky-Ricky into
the bakery. Call the cops or ambulance or
somethin'."

I looked back at that lump of clothes not so much
as puffing up for air.
It wasn't something fresh to see a kid busted
up where the Jives roll money.
Brother try to rise outta rank or
some skank not turnin' 'nough trick,
and it all get real real quick.

But a kid like Ricky-Ricky. That
fool wasn't doing nuthin'.
And I put eyes on Old Man Charlie,
peeking out his window.
The end of a broomstick pressed to his chest.
He wasn't gonna do nuthin'.
He'd let Ricky-Ricky die 'fore get anywhere near
Money Mike 'cause he *owned* that corner.
He owned a lot.

"T," hiss Yo-Yo.

I looked back at him and Catch and Jimmy.
We'd all woke up wanting to feel up some girls,
throw back one of 'em Mexican Cokes
and
play hoop all day.
That was it.
Everything was simple
till we walked a street I was never supposed to be on —
been told never to step to.

"Money Mike ain't gonna play you, fool," say Catch.

Catch was right.
Catch was wrong.
Wrong to leave a good kid like Ricky-Ricky
on the pavement lookin' all flat-fixed.

That just ain't cool.

So there I go.
That first step out from behind the building was real.
Real 'cause I ain't been down that part of West Split
since Money Mike half-killed my ass
eleven months and twenty-three days.
Exact!

I was midway 'cross the street when Jay Ridge
stepped out.

"You crazy, T?" ask Jay Ridge in a whisper. "Get
outta here. Quick. Money Mike spinning loose."

Jay Ridge and me was even.
As even as we could be.
We go back.
We got history that ain't bad.
We got history that ain't good either.

I was shaking, no doubt, but my
legs kept going.
And just when I got up to Ricky-Ricky,
Money Mike's black steel-toed boots stepped
out the Spoon's front door.

Money Mike, he's got some pipes on him.
He could sound off like somethin' deadly.

"What the fuck are you doing here?" he ask.

And he might be slim
but his arms were thick and defined.

The word *Vicious* on one forearm
and *Fucker* on the other.

He had potential.

Jay Ridge tried to cool Money Mike out,
but he was on fire.

And I kneel down to Ricky-Ricky quick.
Couldn't make out his face
'cause he was so wet with blood.

I musta' gone pale 'cause I felt the color float.

"Ricky-Ricky." I shook him. "Get up, you fool."

And the second I looked close at Ricky-Ricky,
to see if he lost his breath,
the quick clunk of those black boots met my face.
And *whoosh*.
Just like that.
The earth spun.

The Guys

I shake open.
Catch and Yo-Yo had me under my arms.
My feet half-stepped, half-dragged.
Jimmy was in front us—he was busted up hard.
His arm at an angle, and it was hurting.

"It's gonna be okay, T," say Jimmy. "You cool, man.
You cool."

But his eyes twisted me panic.

Jimmy was scared.
Deep scared.
Like when his older brother took two in the back
when we was five.

Right then, he had that "my-brother-dying" look.
I tried to say something—anything—
but my words
locked up tight between my throat and lips.

The air was tough to keep.

"Don't you worry, T," say Catch.
"We'll get 'em back sweet. Real sweet for this shit."

I rolled my head one side
and seen Catch—
forward:
P A V E M E N T—
other side:
Yo-Yo.
They both was worked over hard like Jimmy.

"Your face bleedin', Yo-Yo."

"Yeah . . . It a'ight, T," he say,
wincing on every step.

He held on his side, tight.
We came to the edge of a alley.
Jimmy stopped quick.

"We gotta shout to somebody," say Jimmy,
reaching for his cell. "T's fading, Catch.
Think we need to get an ambulance for real, yo."

"Shit," say Catch. "Po-lice last thing I need."

"Po-lice gonna come on no matter what. We
been seen by everyone," Jimmy say.

We all held our wait to see what Catch wanted.
He had become leader somewhere between
the Wooden Spoon and the alley.

"Hey, just get me home," I say. "Monica can
scoot me somewhere. Maybe patch me."

Though I wasn't sure what to patch up.

"Too late for that, T," say Catch. "We way past
that. Shit, y'all! I can't do no time with the Pigs
till I get it all straight in my think. Y'all feel this?"

Jimmy nodded. But where was his basketball?
Where was we? I start looking 'round 'cause
I was mixing it up in my head thick.

"I ain't feelin' sweet, y'all," say Yo-Yo.

"This ain't 'bout you, fat boy," say Catch. "Suck it up!
You—"

"Cut it loose!" say Jimmy. "We got real trouble
at our door."

"You think I don't know we got edge?" Catch say.

My legs buckled. We all sway.

"Whoa," say Jimmy. He got right up on me.

His skin sweatin' so hard.

"Who is you?" Jimmy ask. "Hey. Do you
know who you is?"

"Your arm's crooked, man," I say.

"Who is you!" Catch demanded.

"Theodore," I say, 'cause I was obvious. "Damn,
who else I be?"

The lightness in my head come on deep.
I was helium-filled relaxed.
Like when Catch convince us all to smoke out
after Pinky took the buckle to him
for the first time when Catch was ten.
That weed was laced, and we all lay there
drawn out!

Only, we ain't smoke no weed since.
And I hadn't had any right then, so I was limp
in my think on how I was so loose.

"We was gonna play ball," I say. "Meet up with
some girls. And . . ."

Then I just bust out laughing.
Couldn't tell you why really.
It just all felt funny.

I floated right up into that
Disney-cartoon-blue sky.
I was swimming no doubt.
A w a y . . .
from the smell of piss and beer and
Chinese food.
Trash just be spoiling in the heat.
Man . . .
I was burnin' up!
Sweatin' mad.
The sun—
it just beatin' down on me and lighting up
the whole beautiful-ugly sky.

"Call Trejo," say Catch.

"Serious?" ask Jimmy.

"Trejo too joined out," I say. "He ain't gonna hang."

Jimmy held his wait.

Everything felt so funny, and I just
laugh and say, "Y'all really whipped, yo."

Only, it hurt on my side to be on humor,
but it didn't matter 'cause it was all so funny.

"Just do what I say!" snap Catch. "We ain't
got much else we can do, right?"

"Be settled," Jimmy say. "Hold in."

All quick, I leaned left 'cause
Yo-Yo

threw **up** . . .
chunks and colors and
something look like a cupcake.

"Damn, cream puff," say Catch.

"That's some shit," I say.

Catch held me good 'cause ain't no way I stand
on my own.

"What we gonna do?" say Yo-Yo. "We all in
a mess with this."

Catch's legs shook. He musta barely been
holding his own stand from the way he tremor.
How he hold me up too I just can't know.

"We in a good mess," Yo-Yo say. "I'm scared, y'all."

"What we mess?" I ask. "Catch? Spit it, man."

Catch leaned us up against a wall.
Cool brick eased my sweat-soaked back.

I closed my eyes.

Working it hard
to steady my breath.
I just wanted to pant.

"Trejo on the end," Jimmy say.

"Tell him T got jumped," say Catch.
"Tell him we need the Butcher."

The Butcher?
Catch done gone off his think.
Hell, nah!

Butcher was for brothers gutted
in street war.
Ones that couldn't show up to no hospital
'cause the po-lice front on with questions
no street soldier be answering.
When the po-lice don't get their snitch,
they drop bars to keep 'em calm.
See, po-lice like to cage an animal.
They like to see what it will do.
But even to that bad end, I didn't wanna see
the Butcher.

"Catch." My voice was limp. "I ain't doin' the Butcher.
You feel me? That reject
military fool will mend me up sloppy.
Make me look like a Frankenstein."

Then the words crumbled up in my throat again

and
I
just

d   r   i   f   t   e   d

.

● ● ●

"T!" Jimmy was holding my face. "You fresh? T?"

We were in the streets.
People everywhere.
How we get there?
Why 'em people looking so hard?

Don't know how Catch was dragging me
through everybody.
He looked finished.

All them people.
They was all staring true.

Yo-Yo stumbled, and the three of us swayed.

"Get your fucking balance, fool," say Catch to Yo-Yo.
"We ain't got no time for your soft ass. He spent."

Catch looked over his shoulder.

"Where is that Skin, Jimmy?"

"Be right, Catch," Jimmy answer. "He coming."

I dropped my head
straight

    d
      O
        W
          N.

That's when I seen it!
My gut was bleedin'.
My whole side wet!
How I ain't see that 'fore?

"I'm *dyin'*, Catch. Shit! I'm dyin', man," I say.
My shirt soaked in blood.
In my blood!

"Keep it real, T," Catch say. "Chill that panic shit.
We be there quick."

There?
Where was there?
We was here?
On the streets.
With all 'em eyes unpeeled and—
we weren't in the hood.
We in Browntown.
I smelled pan dulce, cracked corn—

Sirens ripped through the Spanish speak

Then I get set.
Real set.

He was a Pig.
A white Pig.
They track in the dirty
more than any of 'em cops.

"I ain't no banger," I say.

I was cautious of my speak.
You could smell the po-lice
corrupt, looking to smoke a brother out
all over him.

"Officer, he's underage," say this lady nurse
purring 'cross the room.

I gave her curves my time immediate.
She fine to the element of cool!

She walked her sweet-lovely self
over and my head felt
l i g h t . . .
for all the right reasons.
Damn!

She wore the hell outta 'em scrubs.

"What up . . ." I say, thinking I'd work
a li'l handsome man traction.

I'm all teeth and grinning when
she peel back the sheet.
Then she pressed my gut.
And that shit
H   U   R   T   !

"Yo! What's the feel up?" I ask.

She laugh out a bit.
It wasn't funny.
Fo' sure not.

"All right," she say. "On a scale of one to five,
five being the worst, what is your pain level?"

"Ten," I say. "In my heart."

"Ah-huh." She drop the sheet on back.

I'd float forever in that bed
if I got to check on
her every day.
Fo' real.

"Hey, Romance," the cop say. "I need you to explain
how you got worked over like this
and you *weren't* gangbanging."

"Man, I tell you. I ain't no gangbanger.
You see a black man beat up and just jump that
he banging."

"What's that on your hand?" ask the cop.
"Stick-on tattoo? Because that looks like Jive
ink."

I let my arm drop bedside.
It wasn't what he think anyway.
White bread Midwest prick.
I'd done my time in hospital ER before.
Seen cops like him try to make me out thug
'cause I'm black and live in the Split.
He wasn't breaking me on nuthin'.
Not that I done anything to be broke on.

To be real, he wasn't what I had to
worry on right then. That much I knew.
Fo' me to be set up with a bed and
high-up window—7th floor at least—
meant Hilda was gonna be heated.

We couldn't afford no hospital bed and
high-up window view.
Especially with Tony down deep,
Monica about to go and drop that baby any day.
And we ain't locked up any
government health 'cause of taxes or
something on the paperwork wasn't right.

Shit, damn, shit!
What a mess Ricky-Ricky got me into.

"You're lucky the knife didn't go in a couple of

inches higher," say the cop, dropping eyes to
the nurse.

"Leave me out," she say.

And I was mid-grin her way when—

"What in the glory of Heaven were you doing
at the Wooden Spoon?"

And there was nothing more to say 'cause
the natural disaster known as Hilda A. Clark
stood in the doorway, ready to go ten rounds
in a six-round fight.

She marched right fo' me.

Now, I was cut up like a dead fish,
but don't think I didn't make it halfway outta
that bed.

"And look at you," she say, snapping back the
sheet, poking at my sore parts.

"Ouch! Hilda, c'mon." I pushed her off.

Man, was I hurtin' distinct.

"You done got cut up with more
scars," Hilda barked. "Your face wrecked."

It was?

"Mrs. Clark," say the nurse.

But Hilda wouldn't be discouraged.
She was
high heated!
That's the worst kind of being mad for her.

"He gonna look like some damn Frankenstein, ain't he?"
Hilda ask the nurse. "What kind of stitch you droppin'
in this place? Look at his brow."

The nurse couldn't exactly bounce
with Hilda's entrance.
A lot of people were like that with my moms.
She could blow the plates off a counter
with the smack of her thick, cracked fist.

Hilda don't play.
Never!

"I ask you a question." Hilda's eyes drilling
at that pretty sweet nurse.

"I'll get the doctor," say the nurse.

"Who he?" Hilda pointed to the cop.

"Detective Kelly," say the cop.

Hilda coulda busted the floor way
she walked so intent toward that fool.

"You been questioning my boy?" she ask.

"I was here when he woke up, Ms. Clark."

"Mrs. And don't play me the fool with your
soft eyes, Mr. Kelly," she say. "You can sniff
somewheres else."

"Mrs. Clark—"

"Let me clear the noise for you, sir. My son nearly
lost his life today. And whatever questions you have
can wait till he up and pee without a tube in his
man business."

"Huh?" I say.

Not knowing I had a tube in my man business,
I look under the sheet.

"Damn . . . now, that's real," I say.

"Hush it!" Hilda say to me.

"We believe your son witnessed or participated in—"

"You have a warrant for his arrest, Mr. Kelly?"
ask Hilda. "Nah, I didn't think you'd be ready like that."

Hilda did what Hilda do best.
Make like she rip your thought
right outta your head

'fore it ever had a chance
to settle.

"We done, Mr. Kelly? 'Less you plan
to cuff him to the bed. Show all these nice people
up in here how dangerous you decide he is."

Hilda didn't fear cops when she knew she was in
the right. Sometimes I wondered
if she even feared 'em
when she knew she was in the wrong.

"We will be talking to Theodore," he say.

Pig wasn't playin'. It was on. Way on.
I could feel it deep the way he give me look.
Whatever all that went down,
after Money Mike kicked the light outta me,
it wasn't good.

No doubt.
Fo' real!

I needed to talk to the guys.
I needed to know what really up.

"Keep him close," say the cop.

"We ain't planning no cruise to Mexico if
that's what you're fishing."

"Yeah. Okay. Feel better, son," oinked the Pig.

Son?

Whatever, White Bread.
I know how 'em cops work.
I ain't gotta tell 'em nuthin.'
Hell, nah.
Tony spit it solid when we got stepped to
by a couple squad-car Pigs when I was li'l.

He say, "Just keep your cool. You feel?
No need to hold school with those ain't ready to learn."

I useta think Tony coward, but he was
on it wise. Real smart.
He knew what time it was.
He knew the game.

That Detective Kelly wasn't outta the room
three steps when
Hilda turned back at me with all that high
h   e   a   t   .

"You tryin' to end you?" she ask.

"It ain't like that."

"Oh, now you gonna tell me how it's like?"

"No, ma'am, but you ask how it is," I say.

"Theodore Todd, don't *ma'am* me.
I'm hot to your *ma'am.*

It ain't gonna clear you this time.
This is deep and down."

She on with the pacing.
When she was spun tight,
she'd step, getting her hands open
to talk up to the ceiling or sky.
See that's where —

"Your son trying to finish us, Tony Michael,"
she say, looking up. "He on to put us all
down with worry with his fool head sense."

Hilda held conversation with Tony wherever
we be.
Grocery store,
on the bus,
in the kitchen —
nowhere was safe from when she needed
to hold speak with Tony.
Ain't nobody think crazy on it in the Split either.
Everybody knew it was just how she got through.

"He gonna be the nail for every edge
of my coffin," she say, looking up.

"I swear I wasn't looking to dig," I say.

She drop eyes at me like I was a complete half
of half-crazy.

"Then why was you there?" she ask. "When you,

as the Lord and Tony watching from above, *know*
you ain't never to step in that part of the Split."

I held my quiet close.

"You gone half-fool?" she ask.
"I didn't born you to go half-fool, boy."

I dropped my head to the side.
She wasn't gonna like it.

"Me and Catch—Jimmy and Yo-Yo—"

Her hand went up. "Stop right there."
"Hilda—" I say.

"I knew it was those three throwbacks. I told you
last night to cut loose from 'em. Didn't I say
chill that down? They nuthin' but pennies.
Not even nickels or dimes.
Tell me I'm wrong."

"You wrong," I say. "You wrong a lot, lately,
but you ain't gonna listen. Shit."

And there went her thick neck, cocked to the side.
Now we was in the mix.

"You just spit back at me?" she ask, with the kinda
attitude I never wanted to draw. "Speak loud.
'Cause my ears must be off."

She poked at my side.

"Speak it, Theodore Todd."

"Ouch, Hilda."

But she kept on poking.

"Did you spit—?"

"No. I just wanna be on the real."

"I don't think you feelin' me," she say.

"Stop pushin at me," I say. "You ain't got none
of this right. It wasn't the guys who got me in edge.
It was Ricky-Ricky."

She stopped poking at me and started to cool.
Not by much, but I'd take what I could earn.

"Let's get straight quick. 'Cause a lot of word goin' 'round
the Split," she say.

"What kinda word?"

"That you, on the specific, had something to do with
Ricky-Ricky getting dropped."

"Mama, you know me. I don't bring heat, 'specially on
a stutter boy with half-sense. That ain't my cool."

She wasn't sold.

"Look," I say. "We was all straight. No edge.
The guys and me, we was heading out to play ball.
Fo' real."

"Wasn't two days ago Catch got picked up by the
po-lice," she say.

"He almost get pinched," I say. "And you know he
wasn't doin' nuthin'."

"You just focus on why you up in here. You feel me?"

Damn, I just want her to give me relief for once.
She been up on me 'bout Catch and the guys
since the first day school let out.
Tell me I need to make time at the Rec Center.
Hang out and play fun with kids don't have trouble
at their door on the regular.

"I'm not wasting my time with you," she say. "Tell me
what I need to be knowing."

"We was walking by Sweet Pea's when
Ricky-Ricky crossed up to us," I say. "He was on.
Said he had speak fo' Money Mike. Said how
he had something to spit. The guys, they was cracking wise
at him. They think he was floating on firefly or
crack or something. I dunno. He just seemed off.
So, when he take to leave, I got the guys to follow with me
and—"

"Mistake," she say.

"He got jumped something black, Hilda.
Me and the guys saw it."

And I did. See it.
Like all again, right then.
Money Mike dropping rage down on that kid.
Jay Ridge trying to cool Money off Ricky-Ricky.
But Money Mike . . . he was—

"When he wasn't movin', the guys wanted
to roll to the Court," I say. "But . . .
I was the only one went to help."

"And why would you do that?" she ask.

I shook my head.

"Serious?" I ask. "Tony says you always help a man
can't help himself back up."

"Don't bring your father into this."

"I'll bring him!"

"Don't!" she warned.

I held my quiet, but now I was heated!
Heated 'cause Tony woulda done the same.
And I wasn't all truth no lie to her.
Ricky-Ricky wasn't just some stutter boy.

We'd shared days
and sometimes nights when I was li'l,
and she knew that.
And when I got old 'nough to know how he
was touched soft in his head, I drifted from him.
Ain't proud on it.
That's just how it all went.

But after Big Joe got locked down, I
kept eyes on Ricky-Ricky.
'Cause there were some brothers in the hood
try to sweat the kid. Test how far they could shove
him 'fore he quit laughing.

Catch always on me to stay clear of it.
Say it wasn't mine to be responsible.
But Tony always say you stand up
for those can't stand up for themselves yet.

And *yet* just hadn't come to Ricky-Ricky, so
I stood up.

"Go on," she say. "You got something on the
stove. I see from your look that it's cookin' to a boil."

"You know it ain't right to beat down a
kid like Ricky-Ricky. Tony woulda done the same—"

"You finished."

"Nah. I—"

"I didn't present you a question," she say.
"Now you listen to me, Theodore Todd Clark.
Them boys at the Wooden Spoon will *put* you
in the ground. They got no reason not to, given
how you rubbed 'em the first time. You *more* than
know that."

I *more* than knew 'cause
she'd never let me forget.
How I'd busted up her heart good,
thinking I could make right with those guys
who run the Split.
But when I really get how they
turn out li'l slingers barely
old enough to dream, so if they get clipped,
law can't crush 'em on the real, I was done.

But it ain't like some football team or school club.
Not with the Jives.
You can't just be done.
Even if you ain't all in.

"You hearing me?" she ask.

"I *know* it ain't right to leave a guy
laying in the street like that.
'specially a guy like Ricky-Ricky.
And that's where I'm at on it. And I know you
fired up at me. I feel you. But I just couldn't
walk it off."

She held her quiet.

Then I seen it come on her.
She didn't want to let me know
that she knew leaving him was wrong too.

Hilda was a hard woman,
but hard or not she didn't
want to see me get killed.
Not like Tony.
Bullets to the brain,
buying a loaf of bread and a gallon of milk.
She didn't want me
swallowed up by the streets like my brother.
Or stuck like Monica.
She needed—she just . . .

She couldn't take another loss.
She wasn't built of bricks.
Just hot air.
But some pretty damn hot air.
Just so we real about it.

"The world just got a lot harder for you, Theodore," she
say. "It just got real thick. People got eyes on you."

She took seat on the bed.
Man, was she wore out.

"These Pigs. They hungry," she say. "They real hungry."

Pig's stomachs been growling fo' months.
They looking fo' someone to hang up

fo' all the slingin' and scooting and drive-by shooting
up in the Split.
Ain't nobody step up with speak
'cause they 'fraid of getting smoked clean out.

"Mama?"

"What?"

"They help him?" I ask her.

"Who?"

"Ricky-Ricky," I say. "Anybody step to him?"

Her face went long.
Too long.

"I'm sorry, baby," she say. "He ended.
Ambulance come, but they couldn't give him
breath. Mildred's a mess 'bout it. Monica says
she been cryin' and singin' to the ceiling all afternoon.
Sometimes I just don't know what to pray for in that
neighborhood."

I felt myself raging up.
It was just straight-up stupid wrong.
Whole fucking thing.
What the hell was Ricky-Ricky doing there?
Why flat-fix a kid like that?
He ain't got the sense to come out the rain.

I took it in the gut and a boot straight to black
and still . . . he'd died.

And my brother Money Mike had done it

a   g   a   i   n   .

Lockdown

I was mad restless up in
Room 721.

24-hour medical observation was just off.
I was diamond.
I was fire.
Didn't need to be under watch.

Brothers get beat down
fifty-nine times worse
and got their sneaks under
the kitchen table for meal same night.

My phone drizzled out, and I ain't heard

nuthin' from the guys.
Not a thing, and I needed to get up outta
the hospital and know what was going on
with Catch,
Jimmy, and Yo-Yo.
How was they?
Where was they?
What was going on in the Split fo' real?
Why didn't Money Mike cap all three us?
He always carry big heat.

I couldn't just settle out.

Then this woman swallow up all the quiet.
She go to
   S C R E A M I N G
in the room across way.
You think she seen her own death comin'
the way she go on.

She was fierce in her sound.
Old dude stretched out across from me
didn't even make a move. He just keep on
dreamin'.

That woman start to make step into the hall.
Her gown open in the back.
Ain't got no panties on.
Her hair a stringy loud mess.
Like a comb and a night of sleep
hadn't seen her ten years straight.

Nurses bum-rush her with this big-ass
Rent-a-Cop.
Man, that woman was hollering and fighting.

"You can't make me go out!" she say. "Get your
motherfucking hands off me."

I come off the side of the bed
and
struggle to make it up straight.
My head went
right to light, and the walls whirl—

Damn!

Them boots of Money Mike still had me in flight.
My head a c h e .

And that woman cray in her speak on Jesus,
her daddy, and the Devil coming out the TV.

"Now, that's some crazy shit," say Trejo, up in the doorway.

He up taller than when I last see him.
He show up to Tony's funeral in a borrowed suit
and
Converse sneaks.
Say it the last time he gonna say good-bye to anyone
in borrowed clothes.

"You making to walk outta here, Poco?"

"Just takin' a stretch, man. This place is hollow."

I settled back to the bed.
He shut the door.

"This place . . ." he say.

I flipped on the light above
my bed.
Squinted from it being so bright.

"I know, right?" I say.

"My cousin, Hector. You remember him?"

"Fo' sure. He make those mad burgers on the grill.
Those spiced-up fries."

Trejo smile.
He kinda soft fo' a sec.

"Forgot about that, man," Trejo say.
"Memorial Day weekend."

"Two years," I say.

We held our quiet.
That was the weekend that set him and Catch
into fighting.

Set all us apart.

"Anyway, yeah," he say. "Hector's girl got a sister who working nights up in here. She slip me in."

"That's real cool of her," I say.

There was this, I dunno, awkward in between us.
He'd watched his baby sister die up in the hospital.
She kinda kept his heart lit and his eyes soft.
Man, she could blow it out, you know?
Make a whole room just glow with her laugh.
The way she tell stories half-English.
Half-Spanish.
Always full of twists and surprise.
She was a good kid. Always on the follow with
Trejo. It just take one time wrong.
Even if it seem like any other day.
In West Split, it's never any other day.
Fo' real.
Her head got cracked in the middle.
Ain't nuthin' Trejo could do for her.
She went down slow, and he hated on this place.
So, it mean a lot he step here in the night to hold speak.

"How you feelin', Poco?" Trejo ask. "You were looking pale when I dropped you guys."

"I'm on."

"You look off," he say.

"Just need to bust out, man. Hear what's buzzing on the streets."

He drag over a chair.
Settle in.
He got some fresh ink on side of his neck.
A cross with a banner that say Maria Grace.

"Catch and the guys tell you what's on?" he ask.

"My phone's flat-fixed."

"TV?"

"Shit, gotta put a deposit down to make it go."

He laugh.
Me too.

"At least they stitch you, brother," Trejo say.

"Yeah . . ."

He pull his phone out.
Start clicking.

"This thing's hot," say Trejo. "What you guys stepped
into . . . killing a soft kid."

"Man, serious. I don't know the speak, but
I try to help him."

"You clean on my side, no worries. Check it."

He turn his phone to me.

There we was.
Me and Catch. Jimmy and Yo-Yo.
Some fool snapped a pic of us near Ricky-Ricky.
Same fool made sure to smear out
Money and Jay Ridge but leave us three in
clear absolute picture.

"CNN, man. That's some real shit," say Trejo.

"Damn . . . I'm marked."

"You say anything?" Trejo ask. "To the cops?"

"Nah. Nuthin'. They was here. They
hungry no doubt. And Hilda, like, think
I should jet. Down to Texas with my three
good cousins. You believe that? Me. Sportin' some
cowboy hat and saying 'Pardon me, ma'am.'"

We smile on it.

I'd missed our speak.
We went back. Way back.
We had time between us.
But we had to divide when he enlist with the Skins.
He took ink and everything shift.
But when Tony drop, he come to the funeral.
He show when my own brother Money Mike wouldn't.
That was real. That was true.

"She might be on it," say Trejo.

"Nah. I ain't running. I didn't do nuthin'. I
try to help him, Trejo."

Trejo held his quiet.

"Killin' Ricky-Ricky got heat. Big Joe . . . he's
looking to rage. He don't get out for a couple weeks,
but when he step, he gonna step hard. Your brother
crossed the line."

"You think Big Joe come after me?" I ask.

"I don't think so, but I can't know for sure.
But since he down with the Skins, I'll send a message.
Still Texas might not be such a bad thing."

Texas.
No way was I scooting off to way down there.
Leave the guys.
Leave Hilda and Monica.

Next year I even got school classes I ain't hating on.
I don'   how to be me nowhere else.

                    ut with you," I say. "Mexican
                       same without the Mexican."

                          with me like that since

We was brothers from another mother.
Straight.
But skin . . . it's thicker than time — than history.

So, when he stop laughing, I knew he had to go.

Trejo shook it out with me.
His loyalty inked in his hand deeper than mine.

"Keep it low, T," he say. "Keep it real low.
'Cause you ain't clean with Money Mike.
None of you is. He's off the rail."

"Word. Appreciate," I say. "I ain't gonna get in this.
I ain't no soldier."

He roll up outta there.

CNN.
Shit.
That's big.
How we gonna keep quiet on it?
Cops gonna be back fo' certain.

Maybe I should

r   u   n   .

Just Got Real

Hilda come to collect me from the hospital.
She still burnin'.

Trust

on

that!

Burnin' on the hospital bill,
Burnin' on the hood getting heated.
Burnin' on the social worker who gonna be
comin' back 'round to chew on about Monica
and me and our "unstable environment."

She was burnin' on Tony dead,
Money Mike power,
working two jobs,
needing three to get by,
never breaking even,
the Pigs,
the Pigs,
the Pigs being hungry!

"Tony, your boy gonna end us all," she say
to the roof of the bus.

I just kept my hand at my sore side and made
wishes on street tags she'd end her rise soon.

Only she didn't.

I hear it all *all* the way home on the bus.
When the bus let out, I hear it
two blocks, four flight,
stair stomp
to our dump-ass, no-air-condition apartment.
Deep in the heat wave of heat waves.

Hilda still chewing hard when we push in the door.

"Why all the ready?" ask Monica.

Her belly swoll up tight, and somebody else's
baby big-bouncing at her hip.

"Who this?" ask Hilda.

"It's LaQuisha's. Don't sweat it," Monica put eyes on
me. "Hey, Theo."

"What up?" I say.

"LaQuisha who?" Hilda push past Monica.

I drop my phone on the charge
in the kitchen straight quick.

Monica looked me over deep.

"Damn. You really did take it, huh? That picture
Hilda show me put me optimistic. That's sure
off now."

She touch my face.
Run her fingers outside a stitch.

"Yeah, I feel it," I say.

"Monica—"

"I got ears, Hilda," say Monica. "LaQuisha
is that pigeon-toed girl in the apartment
next to Junkie. She hooked up with Pint.
She offered me fifty to sit with Baby Commodore
while she drop eyes on him at juvie."

"Commodore? What a name to doom a
child," say Hilda. "What LaQuisha *need* to drop

eyes on is that counselor woman at the clinic. That
woman trying to help you girls decide right."

It was on now.
Take off the gloves and step in the ring
'cause they were in their corners.
Monica wasn't down about the clinic.
She wasn't 100 percent with keepin' the baby
'cause she think a good family with some green
might make that kid happy-cool with opportunity.
But Hilda wanted her to end that baby 'fore it
hit three months growing.
And she on Monica every day after 'bout
what to do.
How to do.

I cut straight around 'em and didn't waste no time
digging through a box of cookies.

"Hilda, I ain't in a mood—" say Monica.

Hilda dig 'round her purse.
Throw down two bottles of hospital, free prescription pills.
I grinned when I pick 'em up.
Antibiotics were gonna heal me, but Percocet.
That was gonna fly me *right* through the hurt in my side.

"I'm just sayin' 'cause you know I'm right," Hilda
say to Monica. "All that time me and you standing in line
to get you charter schooled level one. Sun doing
its work to cook me inside out. Then you *do* me like

this and end up baking your belly with that no-sense-fool Buffalo's baby."

"You done?" ask Monica.

"I ain't even started," say Hilda. "I may work all day and into the night, but I got time to see how you carry on."

Monica shift the weight of that big Baby Commodore so she could step into Hilda.

"Don't sweat me 'cause Theodore nearly got flat-fixed—again," say Monica.

"I don't wanna be in none of this," I say, popping 'em pill bottles.
Man, my pain ached!

Hilda made off to change for work.

"You steppin' got the news and everyone busy to talk," Monica say to me.

"I seen."

"Cops come by here looking to talk to Hilda," Monica say.

Hilda done stepped out of one work dress and was halfway into a second when she come back in to where we was.

"What she say?" I ask.

"She was at work, so they move their time there.
Man, she was heated."

"I'm still heated," say Hilda, sliding out a kitchen
table chair.

She moving like there were a contest to get out the
door.
Trying to keep her hair in shape.
It just everywhere.

"You musta drank some crazy juice
walk up on that side of the hood," say Monica.

"That's me," I say opening the fridge. "Drinking
crazy juice."

I threw back a swallow of milk outta the jug,
and just as fast

sP I T !

"Shit, y'all. That's off!"

"Theodore, don't you showcase that speak up
in here." Hilda turned to have Monica zip her snug.
"Busted up or not, I'll bend you back."

"Drink the sweet tea," say Monica. "I just took
it from the window."

Hilda freshed up her face fast.
She never take extra time on it anymore.
She didn't want no man but Tony, and Tony dead.

"I got a double shift," Hilda say. "So y'all need to
figure food out together."

Monica put Baby Commodore in a stroller.

"I'm meeting out tonight," Monica say. "Theo,
need to fend."

"No, you isn't," say Hilda. "We got hongry Pigs
in the Split and the Jives wanna end your brother."

I throw back 'em pills with sweet tea.

"I don't need no babysitter, Hilda," I say. "And I gotta
step out too."

Hilda look at me like I was alien.
Hands at her hips.
First time she stopped movin' since we leave the
hospital.
That's the kind of stop movin' that scare a brother deep.

"You need to get real *real* fast, Theo," Hilda snapped.
"Read on the paper."

She hold the newspaper up to me.

"Read on it," she continue. "We all a focus. Social worker

don't need much to put her nose up in this. She already think
you both better off in some foster home."

I eased into a chair 'cause my side thick with pain.
Put eyes and time on the smudged-up headline:

WEST SPLIT YOUTH SLAIN IN GANG VIOLENCE

Detective Kelly and a couple squad Pigs all
huddled around a bloody sheet with li'l nubs
for fingertips sticking up.

There Ricky-Ricky was.
Toe of his right sneak poked out.
I swear, it was wet with blood.

Hilda was busy movin' 'round.
I wasn't paying her attention.
Reading on that article with a pic of the guys
dragging me outta the street.

"I gotta make time," Hilda say. "Only ten minutes to
get twenty minutes across town. Tony, my life gotta
be easier, or I'm gonna drop before I'm forty-three and
come join you. God Almighty be sure. Monica,
please, keep eyes on him."

"I hear you, Hilda. Don't press."

"Theodore?" say Hilda.

"Yeah?" I say, but was fixed to the paper.

"Look at me when I speak," Hilda say. "You stay close. You feel me?"

"I feel," I say.

"All right. Y'all keep it real."

And just like that, Hilda blow out the door—

S L A M !

It startle Baby Commodore.
He go to cryin'.
Monica try to calm him,
but she ain't the best with kids.

"Bring him here," I say. "Other side."

I was holding that kid.
His cheeks wet with fear.
I start making faces and li'l cooing sounds.
Seen Mildred do it I don't even know how many
times with babies she care fo'.

"Ain't no one settle a baby like you, Theo," say
Monica.

"Hell, I'd cry too someone slam doors up 'round me."

He actually pretty cute baby fo' a baby.
But what a name.
No doubt he gonna hear some noise 'bout it.

I put eyes back on the paper.
Ricky-Ricky being dead was somehow more real
seeing it all headline and stuff.
And it ain't like a brother dying in West Split
was new, but the City preach on this new speak.

CLEAN UP ALL OUR STREETS

They slap up these sayings on billboards
mostly near Exit 94.
Off the interstate cutting to the rough parts
like the Split or Browntown.
Big ol' news preach on how
po-lice and City
working to "harmonize" the streets —
curb the crime . . . make people do time.

Shit!
They just wanna have a reason to
rush a brother.
Way things been going lately,
they might not even need a reason.

Few weeks to the day,
these two girls from the hood just making
time on the sidewalk.
Some squad-car Pig pull up next to 'em.
Ask them what they were doing.
They was walkin'.
I mean, shit, that's what people do on the sidewalk.
Cops ask 'em to make explanations.
Broad on the daylight.

And people got up 'bout it.
Mighty Mildred call out what was going down
'cause she put eyes to it.
Do 'em po-lice drive up in the white part of town
and ask
'em girls what they be doing on the sidewalk?

My think go to nah on the quick.

But they be "cleaning" up the streets and all, right?

And I don't hate on all po-lice.
At least I make the effort.
Mostly 'cause Tony say not all of 'em the same,
but some aren't level, so you gotta keep your
sense to you.

And Monica speak that think to me too.
But she come at it from some hard space.
That school she go to.
White kids run down on her.
Say she scholarship — affirmative action —
They tell her, *Black get held back.*
White take flight.

But she better than me 'cause I woulda took
flight right up on their face.
Nah, Monica level.
She even.
She just grin at 'em with teeth real wide
and make 'em grades high.
Ain't no amount of scholarship

give her As in AP chemistry
and Spanish
and
English.
That's all her.

She ain't afraid of their skin or hers.
She ain't afraid of nuthin'.

But when she got played by that punk fool Buffalo,
'em white girls—shit, some sisters too—they
all ready to tear her down.
I seen it cut her deep, but she just keep to
what she know.
She say she makin' it outta the Split.
She gonna live a dream worth havin'.
Truth?
Anyone figure out how to be that, it's my sister.

My side went to burning, and I lean back large
in the chair.
Monica take the baby from me.

"Listen, I need to step after LaQuisha get
back," say Monica. "Can you stay cool for a few?"

Monica was edged up.
Something was cooking her.

"I ain't gonna say nuthin' to Hilda. Step wherever,"
I say.

And then somebody go beating at the door.
We look at each other quick.

"Too early for LaQuisha," Monica say. "She
ain't drop me a text."

I eased up.
Damn, did I hurt.
Grabbed the butcher knife outta the drawer.

Then—
    more
BANGING!

We watched tight.
Real
 tight.

I waved Monica into her room.
Baby Commodore giggled.

"Who is you?" I shout.

My voice shook most definite.

I wasn't ready to fight the Jives or hold more
speak with the po-lice.
I tighten my grip on the knife.

They
    bang
AGAIN!

"It's Yo-Yo, T."

What the hell?

"For real?" Monica say.

I popped the locks loose and swung that
door open wild.
Yo-Yo step back wide 'cause I wave that knife
out big.

"I tell you to knock with the drop," I say.
"I thought you were one of the Jives comin' to
collect on my ass."

I threw the knife up in the sink.
Fool.
I was set to kill him for scaring us weak.

"I'm sorry, man," Yo-Yo say.

He pulled me in — shaking me up with his
big ol' laugh.

"Easy on the squeeze," I say. "My side's
still raw. Kinda like your face. Wow."

"Preach," say Yo-Yo.

Jimmy strut in, new ball under his left arm
whipped up in a cast.
We snap-bump shake.

"You gonna let me drop ink on that cast?" I ask.

"Only if you leave space for the ladies . . ."

"Fo' real?" I ask. "That's how it's gonna be?"

"Women like to touch all over a street-war-mended brother," say Jimmy.

"I guess they gonna be all up on me with this puffy face and busted side," I say.

Yo-Yo bent up into the fridge.

"Who this?" Jimmy ask Monica.

"LaQuisha's. Baby Commodore."

Jimmy's face wrecked confused.

"Like the band?" Jimmy ask.

"Who know? That girl real loose in her thoughts."

"That ain't all," I say.

Jimmy high-fived me direct.

LaQuisha had made turns around the Split.
She was luscious and easy to dip.
Catch and Jimmy share a li'l time with her

last summer.
But they ain't hard enough.
She drawn to brothers carry a lotta edge
and Smokers which is how we ain't never hooked up.
Pint and LaQuisha perfect together.
Except he might end her fo' smiling too quick in
any direction not his.

"This puddin' fresh?" Yo-Yo ask.

I was midspeak when I got an interrupt.

"Brother, you don't need no puddin'," say Catch
comin' in from the hall.

He on the end of a text when he brace himself
in the door, going on, "I'm dyin', Catch. Lord, I'm dyin'."

He half-collapse.
Really workin' the re-create on how I went on
after getting jumped.

"Whatever, fool," I say.

He go to chuckle.

"Shit. You was buggin', T," say Catch. "You was
damp with tears and everything."

He brought it in for a half-hug snap-shake.
Catch had one of 'em big white bandages pressed

up on his face.
Eye swoll up.
Lip ripped hard and puffed.

They was all destroyed.
Look like they come off a battlefield like
in textbooks when we be reading about wars.
Still, it was sure good to see 'em.

"Catch, you know you ain't supposed to be up in
here," Monica say.

"How you's holdin' a baby and got one in the oven,
Ms. College?" ask Catch.

She step right to him.
She was intent.

"You better wipe that grin back before I slap it into
your grave," she say.

And just like that Monica serve his pride up on a
whooped-your-ass plate.

I ain't gonna lie.
Monica got the best outta Tony and Hilda hooking up.
Smarts and sparks.

She got potential.

"Damn, you got fire!" Catch was pleased good

getting her worked. "If you wasn't cookin', girl—"

He reached for her belly, and she slapped his
hand
    fast!

"Cool it," I say to Catch. "Don't disrespect."

"Make your time quick," she say to Catch.
"He lost a lot of color from that cut in his gut."

Monica stepped off into the room she share with Hilda.
Catch whip that grin back on
  full extension
at me.

"Can't believe she bed up with Buffalo. That brother
for sure half-queer."

"Leave it," I say. "She don't need no problems
from you."

Jimmy crushed it back on the couch.

He had it right.
I was feeling that.
I took a stretch next to him.

"How y'all know I was back?" I ask.

"C'mon. Ain't no hush in the Split," say Jimmy,

sketching out some sweet symbols up on his cast.
"Tiny Lewis text Catch when you hit the
block. We kept our cool till Hilda jet. We figure
she be off to the work sooner than later."

"Smart to wait. 'Cause she heated fo' real," I say.
"Why ain't y'all hook a brother up with a holla
in the hospital?"

"Cops, man . . ." say Jimmy. "They been prowling.
Shaking out a lot of loose corners. We just kept our
head down. Much as we can with that picture in the
news."

"I feel that," I say. "Trejo come to hold time at
the hospital last night. Show me us on CNN."

"What Trejo steppin for?" ask Catch.

"He just keepin' me to the know. That's all."

Catch and Trejo didn't hold good time between each
other. Not at all.

When we was kids, Trejo lived in West Split.
Mexicans still do.
It ain't like we all segregated.
We got some white folks and even a few Asians. And
the do-gooder hipsters who run the Rec Center. They
all kinds of people up in there.
We diverse and shit.

Anyway.

We all hung out back then.
Skin would blend, not divide.
But Catch and Trejo got inched with each other
over a girl, and they both fool enough to fight hard
and hold grudge over it.

Yo-Yo finish up his puddin'.
He went to spinning that ol'-school Duncan
yo-yo.
Trick it hard and
mess up!

He don't error up on a trick.
Not on one I know him do with eyes shut.
Yo-Yo shaky-nervous.
He only got that way
when there was something dark burnin'.
Like his daddy, Pinky, beating him so hard
he couldn't lay on his back fo' weeks.

"Thought you's finished," say Yo-Yo. "I was real
scared, T. I was real scared for you, man. You know?"

I make adjust on the couch.
Every which way causing me unease.

"Y'all say anything to the Pigs?" I ask.

"Nuthin' to say," Catch speak.

Yo-Yo went back to tricking.
Tricking easy moves.
Rock the Baby . . . Walkin' the Dog.

But something was loose.

"Hilda on 'bout people talkin'," I say. "Some sayin' I
in with Ricky-Ricky gettin' flat-fixed. Why ain't
y'all set 'em straight?"

Yo-Yo mess up his trick again.

"What's on with you?" I say to Yo-Yo.

"You think I could eat another one of 'em puddin's?"
ask Yo-Yo.

I shrug. "Yeah, man. Go on."

Jimmy gives eyes to Catch.
Catch playin' everything a li'l too cool.

"Shit," say Catch. "You don't gotta invest. People here
know what went down. They be rising. Meeting
going on t'night. People wanna go to war."

"War?" I didn't follow the drop.

Jimmy held up his cast to us.
He drawn out a brother slammin' the rim.

Yo-Yo fidget hard while he eating.

Not sayin' he don't fidget on the regular, but this.
It was definitely not the regular.

"What's with you, Yo-Yo?" I ask him.

Yo-Yo shook his head.
That brother uneasy.
Serious uneasy.

"Some Jives and Jay Ridge got jumped last night,"
say Yo-Yo.

I look hard at the guys.
Took a major set of jewels to step that high.
Jay Ridge was like gold-star streets.

"Who dig?" I ask.

"Don't know, bro," say Jimmy. "They come up
behind hard. The way I hear it. They didn't put eyes
on who it was."

Something wasn't on.
The air just settled in the space
between us strange.
Like when somebody ain't being straight.

"Was it y'all?" I ask.

"My arm bust," say Jimmy. "My mom's had me in
sight all night."

Then why was Yo-Yo missing tricks
and
Catch lookin' the tallest brother in West Split?

"Spit it," I say. "C'mon. Somebody."

"Jay Ridge went down," say Jimmy. "Fierce."

"What?"

I pushed my hurtin'-ass self up on the couch.

The quiet held us hard.
I was real uneasy.

"Somebody flat-fix him?" I ask.

Nobody said nuthin'.

"Is he flat-fixed?" I ask.

Yo-Yo and Catch carry big looks.
Catch lookin' to intimidate him no doubt.

"We ain't put hands on him direct," Yo-Yo say. "But we
weren't too far off."

"You a punk-ass, fat-ass bitch," Catch say to
Yo-Yo.

Catch shoot straight up.

He put hands direct on Yo-Yo.
Jimmy and me try to cool 'em both off.

"Be even, brothers," say Jimmy. "Be cool."

Catch stir into a stare battle with Yo-Yo
'fore he settle back sitting.
Straightening his crumpled T-shirt.

"Trejo drop by the Court yesterday," say
Catch. "I tol' him how they's had you flat.
That they woulda killed you cold if we
didn't jump on 'em."

"That ain't all you said—" say Yo-Yo.

"Shut that speak down, pudge-ass fool."

Yo-Yo go back to spinning that Duncan in a
wicked-whip.

"A'ight. So you just lied," I say. "'Cause
if Money wanted me dead—he want any
us dead—we'd be stretched out cold *right* now.
And y'all know it."

They all stayed too good.
They were holding truth close.

"Spit!" I say to 'em. "'Cause I don't
remember nuthin' 'cept being dragged."

"We pulled a Smoker," say Jimmy.

"We don't carry heat," I say. "We clean. We even."

"They's gonna fucking kill you," Catch say.
"We didn't make it real, but I had to get 'em off you."

Shit!
Shit fuck shit fuck shit fuck **shit** fuck
 s hit!

Pulling heat on Jives.
It just got real.

"We didn't end nobody," say Jimmy. "It was just
show. And be honest, if Catch hadn't pulled a gun, I
dunno, T. None of us be here maybe."

My think go to racing.
I couldn't slow down all the ways this was bad.

"Is Jay Ridge flat-fixed?" I ask.

"Nah," say Catch. "He took a whupping and a
light-ass one at that. Look at us. We look like we
sent to Hell three times to the hour. Why ain't
you care about that?"

"I'm full of care," I say. "But a lot change if a
Jive like Jay Ridge cut down by any us. Or
even 'cause of us."

Didn't matter that Catch hadn't whup Jay Ridge,
and Trejo and the Skins probably did.
We pulled heat on 'em to start.
And word will get back quick that Trejo was
in the Split.
In the Split having ears to whatever Catch tell him.

"Look, you clean. You was laid up flat,
nearly fixed," say Catch. "Ain't nobody gonna put
nuthin' at your door."

Catch been running edge since 'fore school let out.
Taking numbers and making them bend fo' Nacho.
Dealing a little weed out in the 'burbs.
Now carrying a Smoker and pulling it on Jives.
None of this was my cool.

"How many brothers Jay Ridge put down?" ask Catch.

"I hear you, Catch," I say. "I got ears. But . . ."

"Enough!" say Catch. "Enough with this punk-ass
shit!"

"Hey!" Monica step from her room.

Yo-Yo's Duncan tangle.

"There a baby up in this house," she say. "And a heartbroken
woman who been crying below us all night tryin' to
rest. Lower your black-rage volume or step it out
the door."

"We even," I say to Monica. "We cooling it."

I was absolutely lying.
This whole mess fierce.
It was one thing for me to step and try to help
Ricky-Ricky.
But now Jay Ridge and a couple Jives get jumped.
That was unforgivable.
We all marked maybe.
I just couldn't know.

"I'm real and serious, Theo," say Monica.

"I got ears," I say.

Monica cut back into her room.

"We gotta stand big," say Catch.

Catch look to us all thinking we'd rise.
We all just hung in quiet thought.

I ain't no soldier.
I ain't enlisted.
I wasn't fighting nobody's street war.

Catch shot up.

"Serious? They cut my fucking *black* face. Nah.
Hell, nah. I'm gonna bury 'em fuckers.
With or without y'all."

Catch tore up outta my place on the speed.

We all just held our quiet tight.
Then Yo-Yo started spinning his Duncan.

"I better follow up," say Jimmy, making to the door.
"See if I can cool his rise. Hey, T."

"Yeah?" I say.

"I'm glad you ain't finished."

"Me too," I say.

Jimmy cracked that cool, brother-got-game smile
and say, "Maybe we still shake out a couple girls
for you this summer."

I half-laugh 'cause it the best I could come to.

"If we don't get smoked first."

"We figure it," he say. "Always do."

Then he slip out.

And Yo-Yo?
He just kept spinning.
Almost like I wasn't even there.

A part of me wished we was all somewhere else.

'Cause we was going to war.
Whether we wanted it or not.

I was in

d   e   e   p   .

Restless

Monica finally stepped outta the apartment
sometime after
8:30 dark.
Made me swear on Tony's grave
and the word I keep to hold
steady inside till she got back.

But my phone been blowing up
big and heavy all night.
There was a gathering down near
the Court.
Over at Curious Roland's grandpa's church.
People getting together to chew on Ricky-Ricky,
and what's been goin' down in West Split
even before.
No way I was missing that.

So I cut out the building and got four blocks
when the tracks I'd just dropped got hot.
Couple Jive guys were sniffing at my scent.

I cut the corner.
Like immediate.
Roll up in Louie's Bodega already flowing
a text to the guys to let 'em
know I was meeting edge quick.

Jive brothers rolled in hard.
They walked intent.
No mistake.
They had eyes on me. I
didn't want edge.
I didn't want nuthin' to do with their truth.
Sometimes it don't matter what you
want or intend.
It's gonna go how it go.

I push to the back of the store.
Keepin' my pace steady.
Couldn't make like I got fear.
Be cool.
Just be on the cool.
That's all I kept in my think.

"What up, T?" say some Jive I ain't ever
dropped eyes on.

His ink was deep.
'Cross his face.

In his hands and knuckles.
He had age in his eyes.
Definitely done time.
Big time from the hardness in his stance.
Them kind of brothers have a way 'bout
'em.
Like they seen into darkness too long.

"I know you?" I ask.

My knees felt weak.
Half adrenaline.
Half fear all add up to
shit I didn't wanna step near.

"Money Mike wanted to make sure you got
his message."

I look at 'em stupid 'cause they speaking in tongues.

"It ain't my cool—this thing you doing," I say.
"You stepping at me like this."

That's when mystery Jive flashed his Smoker.
Tucked quick and comfortable under his
oversize jacket.
Even if it were 85 degrees outside still,
he the kinda brother don't sweat.

Fearless.
Already dead inside.
Them kinda street brothers

always make my knees loose
in their stance.
They got potential.

Brother Jive with the gun got up on
me close.
This kinda dance end one way,
and I wasn't packing heat.

But fo' truth.
Shit got
R E A L !

The brother everyone call Smokey
snapped the crack back of a shotgun.
It ain't a sound I hear too much.
It was ol' school 'round West Split.
But that sound keep that Jive from
dropping me.

"How we playin' back here, Young Black?"
Smokey ask.

His eyes were persistent on mine.

Brother Jive with the gun froze up stiff.
His fingers bound to be tingling for that
Smoker under his ain't-none-of-us-guys-
'ford-a-jacket-like-that.

"I ask how we playin' back there?"

Smokey repeat. "We playin' fair, right?
'Cause I'm a brother that like it fair."

Smokey never smoke or drink nuthin'.
Seen his sister go crack and his two
brothers drip needle in their stick arms.
He carry a Bible in one hand and
the Devil in the other.
We all call him Smokey 'cause he
the biggest, blackest bear in the hood
that don't sling for his rich.

"Why don't y'all turn to me a bit," say Smokey.
"And keep that hand outta your coat there, Mr. Jive."

Me?
I was froze up straight.
Staring deep at Brother Jive with a gun.
Then . . .
I seen him shift his eyes.
He wasn't gonna pull no heat.
Not right then anyway.

He turn to Smokey, who took stance
like God on Earth if there could be
one.
He was broad-shouldered and big-backed
and people in West Split say he'd
seen war enough in Iraq to know to
keep the peace at home.

He was a rebel-badass hood-brother.
Right then, he the only thing keep a slug
outta my skull.

"Here's how we gonna play this," say
Smokey. "We all gonna keep our cool
'cause we is cool. Mr. Jive, you and your
brothers are gonna step outta my cousin's
fine corner store. You gonna let Money Mike
know you were given the right to go in
one, solid piece. That's complete. We follow?"

"Yeah," say Brother Jive.

Only it was straight clear it wasn't
finished.
Not by the world and back three
times 'round. Maybe four.

"Now, I'm giving you a gift, Mr. Jive.
From the ink on your face, I know
you don't respect much on gifts. I got a
little ink myself, but no need to
go into all that. Right . . . this
is my *one* gift to you. You feel me?"

Ain't no one say nuthin'.

"I say, do you feel me, Mr. Jive?" ask Smokey.

And that's when I seen Smokey go
black in his heart and rage in his eyes.

That look scare a brother Caucasian.

"Because I drop more foot soldiers in the
desert than alive," say Smokey. "And I will
meet you on the battlefield anytime
you come back in this establishment.
I promise you I will meet you in Hell before
I rise to Heaven. We schooled?"

With a nod, Brother Jive and the other
two enlisted stepped for the door.

Brother Jive drop his head back.
Making sure I know
that he know
we wasn't done.

Smokey watched them clear the block
and look back to me. "You nearly met Him,
Young Black. And from what I see, you
wasn't ready."

Smokey gave his cousin the shotgun and walked
straight to the back of the store and made
himself an iced coffee.
Four creams.
Two sugars.
A pinch of pepper.

I didn't know if I was supposed to be
watching or walking.

Jimmy, Catch, and Yo-Yo come running in not too
long after.

"T, you cool?" ask Jimmy.

They was breathing hard.

"Yes, Young Black," say Smokey, sipping that
caffeine, pleased-to-the ceiling and beyond
with his coffee. "You cool?"

"Whatcha want me to say?" I ask.

"Be off him, Smokey," say Catch.

Smokey grin.
Damn, he a Zen brother.

"Settle your step," say Smokey to Catch.
"Streets hot enough without your steam. And
yes, I know you packing."

Catch seem surprise.

"Ain't no secrets in the hood, Brother Rage."

Smokey walk right by me and the guys.
Get up to the door and turn back to us.

"You all coming?" he ask.

"Where?" I ask.

"We mobilizing, Young Black. We about to
raise the hood. Rise."

Smokey took his step on out the
door.

The guys drop eyes on me to hold answers
fo' what just went down.

I don't know why, but I followed Smokey.
Maybe 'cause he caught me curious. Maybe 'cause
I wanted to know what he mean
by

R I S E !

Speak Out

Catch made heavy on the speak for three
and one-half blocks
straight.
Filling me and they guys' ears
with how we needed to get our heads
on payback. How we were
the Power.

Yo-Yo didn't say nuthin' and
Jimmy just say, "I feel you.
I hear you but . . ."

And me?

I just followed ten feet behind Smokey,
who stride through the Split

more fearless than anyone I know not
carrying heat on their back.

Every once in a step, he throw a look to me
over his shoulder.
Go to this grin he must've kept on supply.
That one that say it's all good.
It's all gonna be good.

We come up on the church and people
roaring big on their speak. Nearly slam us
down when we open the door.
It was seriously jammed up packed in there.
Fo' real was it loud!

"We need to hold protest!" shouted one
woman.

　　　　　"This ain't about being peaceful! They
　　　　　killed that soft boy!" say another.

"I'm ready to go drop all them Jives
this sec. Who in?"

　　　　　"The po-lice come by my store,"
　　　　　say Galen from the grocery. "I think they
　　　　　are intent to do something."

"Po-lice . . ." say Janelle Johnson.
"What the po-lice ever do in West Split?"

　　　　　"I'm on that," say a woman. "Trayvon.

Garner. Michael Brown. Gray. Ain't no
po-lice gonna swing anything but death
to any us."

"Streets killed this boy," say Old Man Charlie.
"Maybe streets take back the justice."

Smokey walk through the crowd.
Me and the guys hung back.

"Violence is not our answer," say Smokey.

His step split the crowd down the middle.
His voice get louder each time he say,
"Violence is not our answer."

People hold respect for Smokey.
No doubt.
He ain't rich, but he ain't bust neither.
And what he got he give it in plenty.
People settle their speak.
It was something 'cause he commanded that
room without putting fear into nobody.

"Violence is not our answer," he say, one last time.

Smokey took to the front of the church and stood
like he ready to tell the Gospel.

"This ain't Trayvon Martin," say Smokey.
"God rest his good soul. This ain't how it

was wrote for Mr. Garner. May Heaven have
his pain. This isn't Ferguson. A young
brother taken too soon, too brutal and
too soon. This isn't Baltimore. A troubled
man meet an end he didn't earn."

"Preach!" say a woman in the front.

"I'm not here to hold sermon," say Smokey.
I leave that to the good reverend of this church
on Sunday mornings. The streets are bad.
We all been turning an eye to the drugs and
the guns and the street soldiers holding rent at
Gordon Cemetery. We all come together
tonight to talk us into some kind of
change. Change without guns. Change
without violence. Because violence is not
our answer."

This brother could speak!
He call 'em to a silence.
Pin all dropping and shit.
Even the reverend couldn't drop that kinda quiet.

"Young Black, in the back," say Smokey.

And that's when his eyes meet me and
everyone go to turn.

My stomach went ill.
I didn't like eyes on me. I

wasn't my father, Tony.
I didn't glow when people looked on. I
go pale and sweat.

"Step to us. C'mon," Smokey say,
waving me to the front.

And the way people parted middle for Smokey,
they parted middle for me.

"T," say Catch.

"Just be cool," I tell him, and continue my step.

There.
Up in the front row was Monica.
Oh, and she was on fire 'cause I promised
on Tony's grave that I'd stay stretched out
on my bed reading some book she pull off
the library shelf.
I knew we was gonna have words later.

I stood in next to Smokey with my hoodie up
and drop eyes to everybody lookin'.

"Y'all know Young Black here," say Smokey.
"He tried to speed Ricky-Ricky out of harm's way."

But I hadn't helped Ricky-Ricky.
If I wouldn't been so bent on being cool
with the guys, I woulda stopped Ricky-Ricky

from gettin' anywhere near the Wooden Spoon
and Money Mike and Jay Ridge and them
angry, fool-ass Jives.

And after all that kid had done for me.
After Tony on me to show him cool
'cause a brother like Ricky-Ricky need
kindness in a cruel world.
After knowing his grandma Mildred
and she treat me like I was blood,
I just let them fools turn him out.

I just hung back and watch.

Now he stretched out cold waiting for a casket
and a hole at Gordon Cemetery.

"Young Black, what are your thoughts
on all this?" ask Smokey.

"Fo' real?" I ask.

"Nothing but real, brother. That's why we all here."

Monica make hard eyes at me.
Real damn hard.
The guys.
They was like everyone else.
Waiting for me to hold speak.
Waiting for me to be something like Tony
or

Money Mike
or Hilda
or even Monica.

Who was I?

                "Don't be quiet, Theodore," someone call out
                                     from the church.

I clear my throat.
Their eyes holding time on me.
Seriously, it wasn't my cool.
Standing all up in front of people like that.

"I don't think . . ." I say.

Smokey give me nods.

"I don't think killin' for street war is gonna make
anything more straight," I say. "Black on black . . . it
just shouldn't be our cool. Like, we gotta evolve
past all that, you feel me?"

                  "We feel you, Young Black," say a woman
                                   from the back.

Their eyes was still holdin' on me.
Old Man Charlie, though, he wasn't havin' it.

"But I see," I say, "why you wanna rage up.
I felt that. When my . . . when my dad, Tony, got

ended. When I seen Ricky-Ricky . . . he just laying
so . . . finished. He just didn't glow."

Smokey put his arm over my shoulder.
There was nuthin' uncomfortable about it.
Made me think of Tony for a sec.
If Tony was the size of a bear, that is.

"Young Black and his friends in the back
nearly got flat-fixed finished," say Smokey.
"You feel me? Dying isn't a hard thing to do
on our streets. They could've used Smokers,
but they choose different. We need to unlearn
some of this think on Smokers and rage.
Young Black is here before you all, sayin' that
there's gotta be another way. Violence is not our answer."

And I think he get 'em his way from their
looks. He definitely convert any doubt in my
think to do different right then.

That's when Old Man Charlie take to stand.

"Smokey, you know I got respect for your
thought," say Old Man Charlie. "And I respect
you attempting to make Theodore part of this
truth. No doubt he brave. I didn't even step when
I see it go down. And I be a grown-ass man
for more years than I can hold memory. And that
will be mine to carry."

Old Man Charlie give attention to the crowd.

"But before I come in here tonight, I sat with
Mildred and listen to how her heart torn from
side to side over losing her grandson. I came here
tonight to see who's with me to end this.
Right now. On the moment. We can't keep handing
our community to all this nonsense. We gotta take
what's ours back!"

People got into their speak again.
There was no quiet to be held.
And no matter what Smokey say,
they couldn't be swayed from one way
direct to another.
                              "Cap Money Mike!"
          "Walk to the streets! We got TV on us."
"Burn the Wooden Spoon!"
                    "Po-lice be trying to step to us right."
"You gotta burn shit to get the TV on us, fool!"

"Just be cool . . ."

People was loose in their think.
I didn't know what to do, so I made
to get up outta there.

I wasn't two feet from Smokey
when Monica step to me.
One hand on her belly, the other
clamp on my arm.

"You foolin' me being out here?" she ask.

"I was feelin' caged," I say. "There's too
much buzz to sit 'round."

"You's marked," she say. "You get that?"

"He's still our brother," I say. "He ain't gonna
finish me. He coulda already done me dead."

"So you wise to it all now?" she say. "Two beat downs
and still think he got any kind of time or respect
for you? Do you?"

I didn't have nuthin' fo' her that wasn't gonna
spin her out uneven.

The guys come steppin'.
That sure didn't soothe the burn she was feelin'
seeing them there.

"Y'all call him out?" she ask.

"He grown-ass," say Catch. "He call his own self out
t'night."

Man, if she wasn't so swoll up in that belly, she'da slap
Catch stupid.

"He fifteen. His ass ain't grown," she say.
"You being a year longer don't make you

grown neither. So don't stand there in your large
stance making statements at me. I'm not in the mood."

Jimmy went to make the peace for everybody with his
arms holding space between Monica and Catch. "We
all got eyes on one another's back, Monica," Jimmy
say. "We just wanted to put ears to what's up. Just like
you."

Ever since she got swoll up on accident, she swing
mad at a beat.
You just can't know when her mood gonna shift.
Women's hormones be crazy fo' sure.

"Have your time," Monica say to me. "Then come on home."

"Cool," I say.

"I don't need Hilda in a roar at me. It ain't my cool, you
feel it?"

"We even," I say.

She cut up outta the church while everyone still
biting hard on what need to be done.
How things need to be on the change.

"Your sister is bitter beast," say Catch.

"Respect," I say to him. "She just wants me safe."

"Yeah, I guess . . ." he say.

We was walking to the back when I see this girl.
She ain't no one I ever put eyes on.
She got a stance that don't quit.

I wanted to approach, but Tisha right up next to her.
And Tisha and me didn't have a whole lot of good
history.
Not that she didn't want us to.
She always making step to me that we should
be dating.
But I just can't be down with that.
She got a mean streak up in her.
And she just too busy in her think and up in trend.
Nails, hair, shoes, clothes . . . everything gotta have a
brand on it.
But Tisha's Jimmy's girl's best friend, so I try to
keep it even.
But man, she can exhaust a brother.
Just sayin'.

"Like your speak, T," say Tisha, stepping to us.

She roll 'em breasts a li'l too open to be up
in church.
Might blind the holy right outta every brother in
the room with 'em.

"Thanks . . ." I say, my look making time for the girl
with her.

Now, that girl.
She was soft and hard and look like she got a thought

or two that ain't all on how large a brother roll up
in his wallet.

"Where Gabs?" Jimmy ask.

Yo-Yo inch up on Tisha.
He sweet on her something wrong.

"You know she ain't down with community
action and shit," say Tisha. "Her brothers be making
it good lighting up firefly to the roots. She ain't
gonna hold up no sign and march or shit. Anyways.
Y'all going to Nacho's party?"

"We up on it," say Catch.

This was on the new fo' me.
Thought we'd be laying low.
Seeing how our faces in the news and cops
be prowling the hood.

"Hey," I say to the girl. "I ain't put eyes to you before."

"You doing it now," say Tisha.

"Really?" I ask. "You know you and me ain't like that.
Why you gotta strike at me?"

"Whatever. I ain't got time for your play-around
noise. Nia dis T. T dis Nia. Y'all can go off and
make sweat."

Nia deliver look to Tisha that woulda cut any
brother down.
Fo' real!

"No, you didn't just step like I was whoring with
a guy I don't know who I just met at a gathering
you bring me to," Nia say to Tisha.

"Ladies," say Jimmy. "We all even. We all smooth."

Man, Jimmy could calm a girl fight.
Been one in school right 'fore summer.
He take direct step in the middle and pull these
two girls apart.
Fingernails clawing.
Hair pulling.
Calling each other names that they know their
daddies slap 'em fo'.
Still . . .
Jimmy cool their fierce.

"We gotta jump over to Catch and Yo-Yo's," say
Jimmy. "Tell Gabs I meet her at Nacho's."

I could know straight quick that Tisha inconvenienced.

"Why I got be a message bird?" say Tisha. "You
got a phone. Drop her word."

"Let's burn, Jimmy," say Catch.

"Just offer her speak," say Jimmy to Tisha.

"Yeah, a'ight," she say, eyes in full-out roll.

When we hit the door, I kick attention to Nia.
Smile out real large.
And know this: she didn't give me much,
but I think she into my step.

Me and the guys hit the streets.
They busy,
humming and scratching.
Music be busting out windows.
Brothers running some ball on the Court.
Old ladies extending time in bust-up chairs,
fanning themselves with whatever square
and grab air.

Yo-Yo drop his head right and left.
He was uniquely uneasy,
and I was feelin' it too, so keep my
hoodie up.
Walk shoulders back and chest out.
It all about show, but show all I had.

Crazy Preacher Man stand up on his plastic
bucket.
Every Friday night till Sunday morning
he took the corner of St. Patrick and Vine.
In the name of the Lord,
Jesus,
and
Christ.

Preacher Man tell us how we all Hell-bound.
Talking tall about drugs and fifty-dollar girls.
Read the Scripture and practically howl out
end of days for our souls.

"You need to get right," he say to us. "Judgment
is upon you."

"Only judgment is on your cray-ass mind, Preach,"
say Catch.

Catch throw a couple dollars at him.

"I'm paying you to go down off that bucket," say Catch.

"Cool it," I say.

"Don't get sparked," Catch say, walking off. "Just
having a little fun with him. Shit. Lighten your
load, T. You ain't some Messiah 'cause you just
hold speak in the church."

Catch had done some time.
Not big time but some.
But that ain't what ate at him lately.
Nah, on the recent it was Pinky.
Pinky drop his belt buckle on Catch more and more.
And Catch can take a lotta pain to keep face,
but, I dunno.
Seem like it making him kinda broke up inside.
Like he deficient in his feeling.

And I don't know how to bring him back to caring.

Catch spit flame four more blocks, and
all the way up into the li'l store
we duck in fo' a couple bags of chips.
He on even hotter.
On about his face marked-up permanent,
on about Money Mike beating me,
on about Jive power and reach,
Catch was on!
And he ready to mix cocktails in his
aunt's mason jars, and burn it all down.
Light up
the corner where the hookers seduce time.
The streets where Jives sling.
The garages and houses where Jives kept hours.
And even the Wooden Spoon.

And I couldn't imagine something like the
Wooden Spoon gone.
When we was all li'l, that was the place
where people could linger in a booth
with their kids.
Burgers and pulled pork,
fries and deep-fried apple pies.
Milk shakes and peanut-brownie fudge cake.
It was the yum if ever there be one.
They had this corner window where kids
could roll up on bikes and order up
soft-serve ice cream and nachos and all
kinds a li'l eatin' stuff.

But it wasn't like that no more.
It was a big corner for the Jives now.
And wouldn't have mattered to Catch
if it was the place he come flying out
his mama's business.
It was Jive, and he intent to cause them disruption.

Yo-Yo, Jimmy, and me,
we let Catch go on with his speak, thinking
the talk might wear him cool.
And it seemed like
maybe it had by the time we climb up
the fire escape to Catch and Yo-Yo's.

But we was wrong.

We was so

w   r   o   n   g   .

Watch Out Fo' Pinky

We was all up in the room Yo-Yo and Catch share
with two of their sisters.
Only his sisters out in the living room cutting up
with some kinda carrying on.
Wasn't right to keep
boys and girls pushed up in the same space Hilda
always say. She made sure Monica and I didn't
have to share even if it meant she had to sleep
in the living room some of the time.

But no space was real in Catch and Yo-Yo's
third marriage each family.
And Pinky, he was gonna keep it real on 'em
'cause his ass, worthless no doubt at makin'
any kinda green.

Pinky was Catch's stepdad and wasn't much on
being any kind of the word dad.
He married up with Catch's mom, Jo-Jo,
on account of a settlement she got right after Catch's
dad die.
Between Pinky and Jo-Jo, they spilled that dough
all over Vegas and who knows where else.
That's just how they do.
So, they ain't got nuthin' but that two-bedroom
apartment fo' six people.
That's worse than me and Jimmy got it fo' sure.

I put attention to the door cracked open.
Pinky was talkin' at Catch.
Catch acting like he lost both 'em ears.

"What you got eyes on?" ask Jimmy.

"I think he's drunk, man," I say. "He look like he wobble."

My phone went to going.
Monica.
I 'bout to answer when—
Catch step large up in the room.

"What's the truth, Catch?" ask Jimmy.

Only—
Pinky come big stepping in.
Hittin' the bedroom door open.

His eyes drag to each us.

He made us all on nervous in our think.
Pinky was supposed to work nights.
Got some new job he been sayin'.
We all thought he be out when we come in.

We was wrong.

"You havin' some trouble with my speak?"
Pinky ask Catch.

Pinky definitely flying on some kinda
whiskey and rock.
His teeth had started to loosen.
His smile cracked and crusty.
He a pirate-looking brother ever I seen one.
Stink like one too.

"What you li'l niggas spinning?" ask Pinky.

That spun Catch complete, unabbreviated to

  h e a t e d !

None of us, 'specially Catch, took right to being
called "nigga."
It straight up and down the middle derogatory.
Tony always say that word lower more black men
than any other, and we needed to rise above
the connotation.

Us guys watched Catch swell up.

His chest holding out large.
His jaw even tighter in its cut.

I seen Jo-Jo
putting eyes on us from the kitchen.
She cooking at the stove,
half looking on with what crackling in the skillet,
half up on where we all be.
None of her ready to step and alter Pinky's
mood with Catch.
She either too scared or too dumb to know
she supposed to. I just can't know with Jo-Jo.

Yo-Yo gripped the bed.
His knuckles working to surface. He
knew how to be 'fraid of Pinky.
He had the scars to keep him in remember.

"I say, what you li'l niggas got goin' on?" ask
Pinky.

The brawl between
Pinky and Catch
was anchoring.
They locked up eyes.
Damn . . . did they do it hard.
Real deep!

"We just foolin' up," say Jimmy. "Tryin' to
keep it all settled in this hot. It wear a brother
out, you know."

Pinky hold think to himself.
Nervous-like in how he pop his head to the side.
Then he kinda grin.
My skin went to crawl.

"It's hot as a fat woman in a weddin' dress," Pinky say.

I didn't know what that meant, but I chuckle.

"Fat bitches sweat a lot, you know," he say.

Jimmy sit up solid.
One of Yo-Yo drawing pencils tight in his hand.
He definitely didn't trust the mood.

"Huh . . ." say Pinky.

His attention wander to me.

"That what it is, T? All y'all just foolin' tonight?"

Pinky never had time fo' me.
I was too soft. Said Hilda had
more balls than me. That's 'cause
she kicked his once when he tried
to step fresh at her.
So I was caught surprised by him giving me speak.

"Yeah, Pinky," I say. "We just foolin' up."

"Seen your sister at the corner grocery other night,"

Pinky say. "She sure ripe."

Jimmy look at me.
Yo-Yo too.
Catch was locked on not looking nowhere but Pinky.

"Yeah," I say. "Hilda think she'll drop anytime."

We was tense. No doubt.
My stomach hurt, being in the room with Pinky.
Luck had played us fool-stupid tonight.
Us thinking he not be home.
'Cause Pinky ready to go the distance.
With any us crazy enough to incite him.

He hungry fo' it.

Pinky strut his drunk-high self right up to Catch.
He savor the flavor of being just a li'l bigger
and just a li'l taller than Catch.

"All y'all's regular heroes," say Pinky.

His right hand firm on his rodeo belt buckle.
Pinky useta ride bulls . . . so we told.
Said the buckle was a gift 'cause he could
break any of 'em animals.
14-karat gold.
Only took it off when he showered or whup
up on Catch, Yo-Yo, or the girls.
The imprint fixed into Catch's back.

A white man
riding a bull.
If that wasn't enough to make Catch fierce,
don't know what would.

"Y'all got your pretty black faces"—Pinky chuckle
at Catch—"all over the TV news. In the paper.
Y'all's famous."

"We was just leavin'—" 'Fore Yo-Yo
could finish his speak, Pinky snap to him.

"Sit your black ass all the way back down!"

Pinky turn his eyes and sick heart back to Catch.

"You was supposed to take out the trash. Didn't
your mama tell you three times already? Whole
fucking kitchen smells off."

Catch was so damn heated.
He like one 'em dogs that show teeth.

"You hear me, boy?" ask Pinky.

"I got ears," Catch spit.

We all held our quiet.
Then—

Pinky snap Catch up by the arm.
Yank him with fire 'cross the room.

"You got ears for me still?" Pinky ask.

Jimmy stood without a moment to think clear.

"We all just uneasy, Pinky," say Jimmy. "With
all that's heated at the Wooden Spoon. We just
got caught up. We just—"

"Shut your ass up," Pinky roar at Jimmy.

Yo-Yo was gripping the mattress so hard, his
bones coulda busted outta his skin.

Pinky put focus back on Catch. "You think 'cause
you rollin' up some rank on the street or on the
television, you don't have ears for everything
I say? This is my house, bitch!"

Catch held his eyes on Pinky, who was
undoing his belt.

There we was.
'bout to be witness.
This shit was off,
and Catch wasn't caving.
Brother be defiant.
He hold his stare, daring Pinky to break him.
His back still fresh with hurt from a week since.

Pinky 'bout to strike him down.
I couldn't—

"Let him be, Pinky," I say.

Shit!
How I get up in that?
Pinky caught off.
Ain't gonna lie.
So was I.

"T," Yo-Yo whisper, pleading I keep quiet.

Everyone held their cool then—
Pinky laugh. He laugh so hard.
He laugh so big.
It be haunting me on the spot.

We thought he spun out with such a laugh.
Gone drunk-high crazy.
Jimmy ease.
Laugh a bit with Pinky.

"Listen to you," Pinky say. "Damn, you got
some Money Mike in you, huh?"

I ain't nuthin' like Money Mike.
Mike woulda done cap his ass.
He just that brutal and just that wrong.

Maybe we thought Pinky cooled.
I dunno.
Maybe we didn't.

All I know is it was a mistake.

'Cause that twisted brother swung back
and
S L A M M E D
Catch to the ground.
Facefirst and hard.
Catch lip went to bleedin'.
Pinky got right over top him.

"You ain't so big, boy," say Pinky.
"You ain't so large!"

Jimmy held me back.

Catch rip up off the floor—
tear at Pinky, wild-eyed and rage-filled.
Only for a drunk, worthless fool,
Pinky move

intent.

He threw Catch against the wall
and whipped off that belt.
It slithered through the air and hissed!

"You better fear me, boy!" say Pinky.

The first strike across
Catch's back shook the
three of us.
Catch wailed hard.
But brother just took it.
Didn't even fight on it.

Then five more lashes.
Each one Catch held his quiet better.
Yo-Yo just cried.
Catch may be mean as all to Yo-Yo,
but you wouldn't know it the way Yo-Yo hurt for him
gettin' beat on.

There was something split in Pinky.
Down the middle or maybe to the side.
Didn't matter 'cause it made his angry unleash.

When it was all done, Pinky recoiled his belt
and looped it through his pants.

"Take out the trash," Pinky say to Catch.

Pinky went out as quick as he come in.
Jimmy and me look down at the floor
when we see
blood
sticking to the back of Catch's shirt.

Catch somehow held his stand,
face pressed to the wall.
Then.
Finally.
He let loose a
b r e a t h . . .
he been holding the whole time
it sound like.

Yo-Yo got up off the bed and handed Catch

a T-shirt off the floor.
Catch threw the shirt back up in Yo-Yo's face.

Catch put eyes at me . . .
They was fierce.
It was no easy thing to look at him.

So none of us
d   i   d   .

She Make the Time Go!

Boom,
   boom,
      boom!

The air part from the fire-beast tech rap
DJ Spin drop
as
Me and the guys strut through the door
at Nacho's.

Catch ain't said one thing all the way over
from his place. We ain't say nuthin' neither.
Gotta respect a brother after a beatin' like
that.

Truth.

But Catch light up hard when Nacho
throw him looks from 'cross the room.

Two muscle-hustle brothers holding security
give us the feel-up.
The touch don't thrill me.
From the ache-face Catch making, I know it
don't thrill him neither.

"I see you back in a few," Catch say.

And he step to throw shakes to Nacho.

Algonquin "Nacho" Morris is this
Hawaii boxer brother that got clipped
in the shoulder during a drive-by
somewhere out East. He was 'bout to
do big battle in the ring and lotta people
say he got pierced on purpose.
Say the bets fo' him higher than against.

Maybe that's how it went down.
I just can't know.
Now he deal a li'l, run numbers, and every Friday
night till noon the next day throws a gather, so big
that it occupy two floors his house. Not that it all
mansion, but it got some room.

So long as you keep your Smoker in the car,
you welcomed in the door.

And we come to these parties 'cause ain't much
else to hold time on a Friday night.
Still . . .
I wasn't warm to Catch running numbers for
Nacho.
Catch had a sheet.
He had a few, and that's too many fo' a brother in
West Split with City po-lice being uneasy on the
late.

Security brothers get finished with us.
Nod we can move along into the herd of bodies
set to move just as DJ Spin flip the tune.
Bass jitter-race the walls.
And when you think the whole place gonna
quake down 'round you, music
smooth out to a crazy shake and bump.
DJ Spin fierce in his drop.
No doubt he gonna be large.
His music make you feel stupid-loose in your sway.
He already drop mix way off in Chicago
and New York City.
NYC, yo!

DJ Spin be complete to the even
if he kept that arm poison outta his veins.
It don't seem to cripple him like a lotta brothers,
so maybe he know what I can't.

"What you got eyes for?" say Jimmy.

"Nuthin'," I say.

"So, you aren't worried about Catch in speak with Nacho?"

"What y'all speakin'?" ask Yo-Yo.

"We just holdin' time," I say.

Catch was in complete float.
Making the room his with nods and custom shake.
Drift over to greetings with DJ Spin.
DJ had it soft for Catch.
He'd come from hard times too.
They connect on that.
So when DJ got the moment, he drop notes for
Catch to spit to.
Which generous for a brother on the way up.
But like I say, they in connect.

And Catch say it less and less but
that what he really want.
Rise up outta West Split battling words like he
Tupac or Biggie or N.W.A.
Can't hate on a brother wanna use his words.
Just wish he lay off the illegal shit.

Me and the guys step through
the haze of Mary Jane fogging up the room.
Black lights and club lasers
scattered toward the main dance space.

It
was
P A C K E D !

And not a whole lotta sweat to be made with
all those people
'cause Nacho kept the temp at 67 degrees 24/7.

Nacho's own Sweet Hereafter bowl
(gin, punch, mangoes, and sweet Everclear loose)
was near empty on the drink table.

Energy drink cans covered the floors.
People was drunk, high, and speeding through
the night.
One DJ Spin song at a time, they all
grind and sway.

It
was
O N !

And way things in the Split, we all needed the
distract.

"This place is on," say Jimmy, crackling off a
text to Gabs. "DJ Spin is dropping truth."

Yo-Yo whip off that Duncan.
We could all be pissing and he'd have one hand
on that yo-yo spinning tricks and still not get
piss on his sneaks.

"What's got your mind, T?" ask Jimmy.

"Catch acting all the joy here," I say. "Like nuthin'
went down."

"That kinda buckle beat would defeat me," Jimmy say.
"But Catch . . . just let it all chill. And try to be easy.
Nobody gonna bring heat up in Nacho's.
It's like, uh, Sweden. Neutral Territory."

I look at him like he straight fool.

"Switzerland," I say.

"Whatever. We all good."

Jimmy snap up a bottle of beer and toss it to
me.

"Just be cool," he say. "And keep eyes for my woman."

Last thing I had going was to keep eyes out for Gabs.
Man, that girl could break my incentive to date women.
She all about Gabs in a way I couldn't get down with.
Fo' sure.

My phone go to buzzing.
Monica.
If I pick up and tell her where I is, she rip whatever
youth still in me.
I kicked it to voice and disappeared it in my pocket.
Didn't want think on the call or her four texts.
Jimmy right.

I just need to
e a s e .

"You could have your pick," say Jimmy to me.

"Yeah. How you figure this?"

"Look at these ladies. See that girl over there? She
makin' time for you."

"Shut that shit down." I laugh.

Wave off his fool thought.

"Serious," say Jimmy.

He look on to Yo-Yo.

"Yo-Yo, ain't these girls makin' time T's way?"

"Yeah, sure," say Yo-Yo, who all eyes on the trick he spinning.

"T, you a hero to 'em," say Jimmy. "You up
in the paper and TV. They know you step
to help Ricky-Ricky. Not a girl up in here don't
wanna make you her snuggle brother."

"Snuggle brother, huh?" I say. "That's tough."

Jimmy's girl Gabs crash up beside him with a
few her posse of trend girls, including Tisha.

Gabs was serious glamour tonight
with her hair did swirl up.
She always make herself up big but this 'do had
noise!
Her clothes.
Her nails.
She wear a wallet out *fast.*

Jimmy work mad hours at
Fast Guys Chicken Shack
to afford Gabs a few sparkle things.
Not that she didn't have spare green from her
brothers running firefly to all the South Pear kids.
It was Jimmy's pride to afford her, though.

I told him straight up when he first sayin' he
gonna step to Gabs to think on it absolute.
'Cause you gotta be half-fool to be with a girl
as dangerous she is.

And
every
brother
know it!

She got five brothers.
Three serving big time, but they all connected
on the outside and got angles every which way
you make 'em.

Jimmy see something special in Gabs.

No clue what that be.
But you can't crush on a brother's view.

"She's degenerate in her thought," Gabs tell Tisha.

They got eyes on some girl curling up on DJ Spin.

Tisha say, "Serious. No lie."

"Where you been, baby?" say Jimmy to Gabs. "I
been dropping letters to you for a while."

"Awwww. I'm sorry, my man of cool. I just making
time to get ready for you. You like?"

She do a step-back, showcasing all her curves.
Jimmy smile go wide.
"I ain't mad at it," he say.

"You ain't . . ." she say, and fo' real, drop tongue
all up in Jimmy
and
grab his Man.

Damn!
She got no limit.

Yo-Yo step to draw Tisha in with one of his
yo-yo tricks.

"What you think?" he ask Tisha.

"I think you supposed to be a grown-ass man
and not be playing with toys."

That cut him up the middle.

Yo-Yo wander off to hold time with the chips.

"Why you gotta do him like that?" I say to Tisha.
"He sweet on you."

"That don't mean I gotta be sweet back. I give
you all the time for this dark, delicious juice
and you wanna rub sweat with my cousin."

"Cousin?"

"Nia," she say. "Why you act surprised? We almost
twins."

Where was they almost anything?
Tisha breed hard curves and more makeup and perfume
than *any* girl should damage.

Nia, though.
She took all the right space.
And there was something.
I dunno. She was definitely more than spark.

She was fire!

A girl whose fire can set everything 'round her into motion.

Monica was fire, only she my sister, and seriously,
I *don't* be thinking on my sister.

When Gabs done making on Jimmy, she
right back at it with her speak to Tisha.

"Look at her go. All on DJ like that. She wears
me with her cheap-ass nails and bow weave."

Tisha sip her drink. "She done expired her meter."

"What you mean? Expire her meter?" ask Gabs.
"You done eat stupid for dinner?"

"Just sayin'."

"Well, you can quit *sayin'* like you knowing.
Ain't nuttin' more tellin' than spittin' out dumb-
ass words on what you ain't know. Can't
know."

I couldn't stand Gabs fo' nuttin'.
She ended my patience 'fore it ever really start.
But she Jimmy's girl and that's all I kept sayin'
to myself.

"A'ight, a'ight," say Tisha. "You ain't gotta
spin me like that. We even, G."

"Hey, T," say Gabs, hanging on Jimmy. "I hear
you meet Tisha's cousin at the church t'night."

"Yeah . . ." I say, maintaining my cool.

Gabs like to chew on a preference.
Make it her gossip.

"He got big eyes on her chest," say Tisha.

"You being fool," I say to Tisha.

Gabs was setting in her hungry.

"So, you like that Atlanta drab-ass kinda girl,"
say Gabs. "That's good to hear. I was 'bout to column
you queer."

"The jury still deciding," say Tisha.

"Y'all beat in your think," I say. "Brother don't drop
his stick in every loose-legged chick, and he bent."

Gabs straightened herself to battle.
Waving her hands all big and bold.

"I know you weren't making me out to be loose-
legged," say Gabs.

Whatever.
I didn't have time for her done-up face and
clear-brace grill.

"Baby," Jimmy say to Gabs. "T just got loose

from the hospital. His head's still sore.
Cut him some time. His think cloudy."

She hold her stance.
Then nod.
Puckering those two-tone lipstick lips.

"We even," she say.

Only I knew we really ain't, but it's all good.

Jimmy point 'cross the room.
Nia was steppin' between the crowd.
Tall can of Mountain Dew in hand.

I drop Jimmy a bump snap-shake and step.

Lookin' at Nia, my head just drift.
Didn't think about the pain in my side
or the stitch in my face.

She was every kind of
F   I   N   E

     FINE
      !

The room go boom every step I inch her way.

"Hey, you go—?" I say.

"What?" She struggle to make my word.

We was right up on the speakers. I
motioned fo' us to move.
We peel through the shiftin' shake of people
in groove to get to a softer space to hold speak.

"Hey . . ." she say.

"I'm Theodore. Tisha throw me intro as T 'cause
everyone nick me that."

"Theodore sounds a lot better."

"Guess . . ."

We was still for a bit.
Sometimes I talk a big game, but when it get real, I
sweat it. And she was making me sweat hard with
her confidence.

"I like your speak out at the church," say Nia. "Not
what I would've expected when you first stepped."

"How you expect?" I ask.

"You dress a li'l thugging."

"'Cause I got baggy shorts? Have pride in keepin'
my sneaks clean?"

"I ain't crumbling your attire. Just saying. You
worked over on your face. You step hoodie up
on your head. Ink laid strong on your hand."

Damn, that mark draw eyes.

"I'm just sayin'," she continue. "Might think you
the kind of brother carry heat on your back."

"That what you into?" I ask. "Brothers with guns?"

She tease the lip of that can with her finger.

"I don't step anywhere with a brother that carry heat,"
she say. "It ain't my cool. Ever."

"Me neither," I say. "I mean heat. Not brothers."

She bust out smile.
It put my stomach to twitching.

"Where is you?" I say. "I mean, you from Atlanta?
That's what Gabs was sayin'."

"Yeah. My mom and I came to share time
for the Fourth."

"Fo' real?" I ask.

"Yeah . . . ?" she say.

"Look, I'm sorry. It's just . . . you come all the way
from Atlanta to visit West Split? That's just—we in
the hood. You on that, right?"

"Really? Oh, hell, nah. We are? My goodness. I

better check myself into the South Pear suburbs
before someone break hard times my way."

"A'ight, I see you havin' a li'l fun at me."

She smile undeniable . . . ripe!
I lose all the cool I keep in stockpile.
My head nod with the music more like some
fidget Yo-Yo get 'round Tisha.
Nia see it too.

"I ain't fool to the world just 'cause I come from Atlanta,"
she say. "We got hood there too. Hoods all over, Theodore."

"Yeah, I just—"

She look past me.
Tisha and some of the crew wave to Nia to
make time.

"I gotta jet," she say.

She get a few steps off, and I chase after her.

"Nia, wait," I say.

She hold a moment for me.
I had no idea what to say to this girl.
My shit was rattled.

"I wanna holla at you," I say. "You be down?"

"Guess we'll see."

And just like that.
She spun right outta the mix of bodies
in move.

Tisha and two other girls.
They was throwing
eyes and giggles my way.
No doubt Tisha gonna try to bend
the truth to fit her mood with Nia.

I look fo' Jimmy, and he set up on the
couch making time with Gabs.

Yo-Yo wasn't nowhere in view, so I make
steps to hold time with Catch.

I kept my head high and my hood down
up the stairs.
Nacho comin' down from the top
and call my attention to him.

"My man Theo," he say.

He brung me in fo' a hug right there
on the stair even with all them people 'round.

"You got people activated," he say. "Making
them wanna grow the concrete green with life."

I didn't follow too easy on this personal joy

he having.
I mean, that brother's eyes,
they was three flights up that house Deep Baked.
Nacho a spark guy.
No doubt.
He big on the shoulders and broad in the chest.
Girls rub up on him without being paid.
But he bake real hard and was loose in his speak.

"You helping that retard—" he say.

But right then, I wish I could kick him in his Man.

"You can't make a better story. You know?" he ask.

He just held eyes to me.
People cut up behind me to get up the stairs.

"So . . . ?" he ask.

"Yeah . . . ?"

"What you going do now?" he ask.

His phone went to ringing.
He hold look on it.

"It's my mama," he say.

That was straight-up some false speak if I ever
heard it.

Catch say when "mama" call, it mean a
number run to Nacho's favor.
Big favor.
"So," say Nacho, "what you got planned?"

"Jus' hang with the guys," I say. "Step to put
eyes on the fireworks in a few days. Jus' stay
outta anything that's not cool."

Nacho grin so wild and big.
His polished teeth practically glow.

"You in a good position," say Nacho. "You could
make a few dollars. People like your face."

With Nacho, you don't gotta enlist.
No ink.
No shooting nobody.
You just gotta do what he say when he say.
And if you keep loyal, he got time.
He always got time for loyal.

I didn't trust him.

"I appreciate," I say. "Fo' real. See my moms
and my sister, they need me to keep it clear.
You feel me?"

He just laugh and slap me up the shoulder like
we been bests forever.
He got strength and knock me off my balance.

"Whoa . . ." he say, helping me steady.

Damn!
My side ache.
I needed to get up on another one of 'em pain pills.

"Listen," he say. "You heal up that side. Let your
purple face get back to black. And if you have a change
in your thought, I got time for you."

"Thanks, Nacho."

"Your man Catch set up in the big bathroom with
Winslow."

Nacho went on down the stairs.
Greeting people all politician-style.
He knew how to work all the angles.

I jog it up and step down the hall.
The needle drugs and powder usually happen
on the second floor.
It also where Smalls Winslow drop ink.
And I knew Catch was wanting some.

Everybody crowded the door intent.
I only make the top of Smalls's 'fro 'cause he
hunched and inking.
Truth is there ain't much to see of Smalls Winslow.
I ain't never known a guy who grown and be
as tiny as he be.
Ain't no one dig on him 'bout to any of my know

'cause he earn respect back when he was twelve
and a few days.
Story go he drop masterful lines on Big Joe and some
of his crew.
So, where his height stop him, his ink drop prop him.

He hold shop outta his mama's garage fo' years
till a popular magazine run a story of his color drops
on some white-boy rapper.
He couldn't keep up when all that business start comin'.
So he go legit on Strawberry Hill Lane.
The street that divide
the hood from the good
as lotta South Pear speak it.

Smalls always stick ink at Nacho's parties.
He liked the bake and the liquor and sometimes
he bring up celebrities to hang out.
And he always cut hood brothers a special
at the parties 'cause he feel they made him.

When I see it's Catch sitting for Smalls, I
slide my way through everybody.

"What up, T?" some brother say,
only I ain't never put time on him. "Real cool
how you try to do."

"Thanks," I say.

I step and put eyes to Catch's arm thick in ink outline.
There . . . mapped into his skin—

"What you think, T?" ask Catch.

M O N S T E R

I think Catch in edge. I
think we all was.
We just couldn't know it yet.
Not in the way that would make me know to

r   u   n   .

We Just Need to Ease

Catch, Yo-Yo, and me,
we was walking tall and shoulder strong
down the street.
It was one something in the morning,
and we got some chicken and sides on the go
'cause they be shutting shop.

We'd cut out the party after Jimmy
made off with Gabs to roll in the backseat of her car.

Being with Gabs mean Jimmy didn't have to worry on
attracting no kind of edge, which soothe all us.
Not even the Jives touch Jimmy on accounta her connect.
That would be straight up and down suicide.

That new ink had Catch pumped.

He lit up high on it.
Fo' real.
He walk taller just having it.
Grinning at the bold-ass letters and smoke swirling
at the edges.
Smalls had done Catch a solid.
Only cost him $50 green.

We come up on this CONDEMNED BY THE CITY
boarded-up crack/smack house.
We kinda claim it when school get loose fo' summer.
Catch say it was somewhere we could just vanish
when we didn't want eyes on us.
He even brung one of those inflatable pool things
to sleep on.

We cut 'round the back.
I run the combination to the lock we dropped
on the cellar door.
Yo-Yo was already digging into the food.
Catch didn't even sweat him.
He too lit on that tattoo.

We all tear through the steps and weave up to the
front floor.

Yo-Yo pass sodas 'round that we keep in a cooler.

"Hit me some okra," say Catch,
taking seat up near the couch.

I toss him the box.

Can't hold seat on the couch 'cause
we had to throw the cushions out
straight immediate. Somebody had pissed all over 'em.

It

  was

     r o u g h !

Yo-Yo beat through the mashed potatoes,
extra-large-size.
Brother could eat like nobody.
I don't even know if he ever really hungry.
It just how he do with food.

I eased down on a sheet we keep on the floor.
The place be run down to the extremes and
rats and roaches find time between the walls,
but it beat being on the streets.
And it most definitely beat going home
and Monica bust my ears to deaf with her speak.
She quit callin' two hours back,
which mean she *real* mad!

"You guys gonna go home tonight?" I ask.

Yo-Yo look to Catch for some answer.

"Nah," Catch say. "We holdin' up in here. How
'bout you? Monica give you ring?"

"Yeah," I say. "A lot of 'em. I'll step that way
in a few. I just can't hear on it yet."

Catch lay a Smoker on the floor.
It was serious heat.

"That loaded?" I ask.

He kinda grin. "What you think?"

Heat make me nervous.
When brothers carry it.
When cops carry it.
Especially when Catch carry it.
It just ain't my cool.

Never held a piece.
Never will.

Tony tell me, "Never carry a Smoker 'less you got
no other choice. You in the government's army, you
got no choice. You wear a badge, same truth.
Otherwise, it makes too many decisions for a brother
he can't undo."

"Where you get that?" I ask Catch.

"Nacho."

"Fo' real?" I say. "You runnin' numbers. Not bodies."

"He call it an upgrade from what I pull the other day
at the Wooden Spoon," Catch say. "He say a tall brother
need to carry a tall piece. Say it send a message."

The message it sending didn't soothe my mood.
That was Glock heat. The kinda Smoker fo' brothers
committed to being dangerous.
They pull that kinda heat, and you just know they
got no problem seeing you go.
No problem at all.

"You know, if you in need of a gun —"

"Don't speak it," I say, cutting his word. "I ain't
feeling that."

"I might," say Yo-Yo.

"Shut your fat mouth," say Catch. "You pop your dick
off, carrying heat."

Catch tossed what left of the fried okra between me and
Yo-Yo.

"I'm gonna drop off upstairs," say Catch.

It hurt watchin' him make to his up.
I seen blood comin' through his T-shirt
from where Pinky beat on him.

He grab the Smoker and struggle to slide it
in the back of his jeans.

"Y'all holla big if anything come knocking," say Catch.

"Fo' real," I say. "Hey . . ."

He hold time for a moment.

"Maybe you could lose that clip," I say.

"Maybe you could give me some ease," he say.

Then he turn and disappear in the dark.
The creek and crack crunch under his sneaks
when he hit the stairs.
The outline of him there then gone.

Yo-Yo crunch on a fried pie.

"We got another one of those?" I ask.

Yo-Yo scatters through the bag and hands me one.

"He worried about you, T," say Yo-Yo.

"Catch always wanted to carry heat."

"Yeah, maybe. But he didn't ask for no upgrade gun.
Nacho push it on him at the party. He sell it on him like
it critical."

"You think it is?" I ask.

"Seriously, I don't know," say Yo-Yo. "But I seen
him with that first gun. The one he drop fear with

at the Wooden Spoon. He walked around our room
trying to hold it hard. Practicing tuff. You know, fake-dropping
somebody. But . . . I think he scared of that new Smoker.
I know I am."

"Why you think he play it cool in front us?" I ask. "We all
tight. We real with our speak, mostly."

Yo-Yo shrugged.

We held our quiet.
Eat on our pies.

"I been thinking," say Yo-Yo. "Maybe we should all
make a bag and go somewhere south. Maybe Florida.
They got time for us in Florida. They got beaches. They
got girls more fine than Tisha."

"They got gators down there too," I say, grinning.

He got fo' real serious.

"Won't be so much trouble there, T," say Yo-Yo.

"Don't you think there be edge everywhere, man?" I ask.

Yo-Yo face go tight.
His brow deep in think.

"It's like I think . . ." say Yo-Yo. "We gonna get swallowed
here. Right into the cracks on the Court. And ain't nobody
gonna care 'cause we just black kids from West Split.

Brothers get dropped on the day. It's too regular. And the
po-lice looking for a pin for what happen with Ricky-Ricky.
We in a mixed-mess."

No way to be in disagree with Yo-Yo.
He taken the truth to the real.
But Tony. I think a lot on him these hot days.
I know Tony wouldn't accept that's how it all had
to be wrote. Us guys on the run?
That didn't make any kind of right sense.

"I bet it's nice up in Florida," say Yo-Yo.

"Don't matter where we go," I say. "We ain't got 'nough
money fo' four burgers and Cokes. Jimmy the only one
got a job. And he ain't gonna skip out on his mama.
Shit. They the only one's I know that get along. That's too
good a thing. He shouldn't have to run."

"Then the three us," say Yo-Yo. "I've been putting back
every green I touch. Every time Pinky pass out for long
stretch, I lift a little."

"Are you fool? He end you."

Yo-Yo shake his head.

"Of all the things he think on, where his money go ain't
one of them, man," he say.

"How much you sitting?" I ask.

Yo-Yo held his quiet.
Rock back and to the front some.
Street light streaking his face.

"One thousand and ninety-two dollars, fifty-three cents."

"Are you serious?!"

"*Shhh . . .*" Yo-Yo cover my mouth. "Be cool, T."

"Sorry, brother, but that is a real number."

Yo-Yo took to standing. He
go to spin his Duncan.
Couldn't really see it.
Just the whip and burn of it tricking on the
string.

For a sec, I think on Nia, but I just couldn't
hold up there.

My mind set up wild-busy on all kinds of think.
On the people at the speak-out in the church.
On that cop at the hospital.
On that summer reading Monica on me to do.
On Hilda working two jobs.
On Money Mike ending Ricky-Ricky.
On
and
  ON
    and
      ON!

It was a million plus one TV screens up in my head.
All with some other kinda story running.
Then—

Yo-Yo stop his spin.

"So, what you think?" he ask.

"We can't run—"

"We gotta get outta here," Yo-Yo say. "We finished if we
don't. There's too much potential. You know?"

I lean back on my hands.
Staring at the tag Yo-Yo drop on the wall
first week of summer.

BROTHERS FOR LIFE

"We in a fine mess," Yo-Yo says. "Catch gets hotter every
second. You see how he does. And you marked—"

"That ain't certain."

He throw me a look. Who was I foolin'?
I was probably marked the minute I crossed the street
to help Ricky-Ricky.
Still.
It wasn't official and being marked is something
Money Mike like to make official.

"What you think, T? You think we could cut out?"

"Look, I feel you," I say. "But . . . I mean we got school come August. I got Hilda and Monica. She cooking that baby big in her belly. Shit, what 'bout your sisters?"

"I don't know! I don't know about anybody else!"

And Yo-Yo stop the time on that.
Cut me quiet.

He terrified.

He scared on like a Smoker pointed direct to his head.

"Hey!" shout Catch from upstairs. "Y'all straight?"

"We even," I call back.

Yo-Yo pace mad on the floor.

"They got me scared, T," say Yo-Yo. "When they had you almost flat-fixed."

"But I ain't—"

"Yeah, but you nearly was. Us beat down. It ain't how I see it. I can't. I wanna tag up walls. Make comic books and shit . . . I just . . ."

"C'mon. Sit it out."

"Ain't nowhere to go, T." His voice crumble.
"Can't go home. Can't stay on the streets. Nowhere safe."

"Man, be cool. Sit it out," I say.

Yo-Yo dropped, cross-legged.
He so agitated. Real itchy.

"Think on this," I say. "When I got beat fool-crazy for
not enlisting with the Jives, we all pull together, right?"

He give me a nod.

"This is just another one of 'em times. We just gotta
stick like truth to each other. Nuthin' touch us then.
A'ight, man?"

He didn't say nuthin' else.
Not 'cause it wasn't percolating in his thought.
Probably because we both knew I just made
something up,
so we wouldn't have to think about running.
So we wouldn't have to think about dying.

So we could both be easy and sleep a

f   e   w   .

City, Wake Up!

Sirens
rip through the walls.
Squeal!

My phone blew up not even half past
6 a.m.
Noise from the street drop faint
as I force to squeeze my busted-tired eyes
to make out the words on the screen.

First it was Monica.
Then it was Hilda 'cause Monica
done spilled that I wasn't home.
Hilda still on shift threatening to break

me in two clean halves if I don't bust my back
to get on home.

Damn . . .
Both of 'em at me hard and deep way too early
in the mornin'.

I lean up, and it caught me off that Catch
was holding watch at me and Yo-Yo's sneaks.
Knees drawn tight, he was propped with the gun
in his hand.
He easy with that Smoker in a way that made me
squirm inside.

"Your moms?" ask Catch.

"Yeah . . . she on it early. Monica too. Thought I set
my alarm."

"You did," he say.

I kick into my sneaks.

"You sleep right through it," he say.

"I gotta make time," I say. "Hilda ready to
close me."

He stand big. "I walk you there."

"Nah, man. I'm solid. Ain't nobody lookin' to
dig this early."

I made for the cellar.

"I'm gonna give you steps," he say, coming
up behind me. "Need to stretch my back. Get
some pickings at the bodega."

I climbed out and shook the sleep outta my
eyes.

We didn't say nuthin' first few blocks. We
seem to have less and less to say all summer.
Ever since Pinky went harder with the rage,
Catch he just—meaner 'bout
most everything.

"I been working on some spit," he say.

"Yeah? You ain't say nuthin' 'bout new spit."

"I keepin' it still, ya know," he say. "Didn't wanna
presume it was gonna evolve into somethin'. But
DJ Spin put some ears to it. Say he wanna
record a few tracks. Wants to test it on some clubs
and with some of these music producer guys."

"That's tight, man."

He chuckle.

"Would be some shit, yo," he say. "Drop spit to stay legit."

"Whatever it take," I say.

Dumpster-stuffed stench caught a ride on
that sticky flat air already heating.
It gonna be a long damn hot day.
You could just feel it coming.

"Whatcha got going today?" ask Catch.

"Dunno, man," I say. "Maybe lay low a bit.
Sleep. Read a little."

"Joe College, huh?" he say. "Theodore Todd
dreaming of Ivy Leagues."

"Why you gotta tear?"

He held his quiet close.

"Serious?" I ask. "Every time any us talk 'bout
somethin' that ain't hood, you get uneven."

He stop his pace.

"Who is you, T?"

"Please?"

"Who is you?" he ask.

"I am who I is."

He shake his head.
Standing like he all knowing on something
I can't.

"Nah. You a black man with a mama working two jobs
and a swoll-up sister. You better start thinking like me
and earn some cash doing favor for Nacho."

"You just on about spitting. Going legit."

"That's talk," he say. "This is on the real."

He kick a beer can in the gutter.
Chase up on it.
Kicking and kicking.

"I ain't gonna sling fo' nobody," I say to him.
"We got enough young brothers doing time fo'
Nacho, Money Mike—all that allegiance to the
hood shit. We just juice poison in our people."

"Shit," say Catch. "I dime-bag and firefly-drop
almost ninety percent up in South Pear. Ain't nuthin' but
white kids and Oreos listening to pop rap thinkin'
they spark."

He missing the truth.
He so into his misalign think.

"Don't matter if you sling it on this side of the city or
on South Pear," I say.

Catch just laugh. Big and full and with no holding back.
Pointing at me like I come at him with the foolest string
of sentences ever.

Ain't gonna lie.
It was starting to burn me.
Way he always holding up—funning at me.

"You know, cool," I say. "You put me on the stage fo'
jokes. But when it go down, I'm the one who crossed
that street to help Ricky-Ricky. I'm the one care 'bout
the hood. I ain't hiding behind no Smoker."

And that shut his big-ass funning down.
He wasn't laughing to none of that.

"What you say?" Catch ask.

I held my cool.
I never hold speak with Catch so original.
He as stunned as me.

"You callin' me coward?" ask Catch.

"Nah . . ." I say. "Just wish Pinky hadn't beat out your
heart through your back, fool."

He charge me hard. Slam my shoulders.
I stutter-stepped, reached for my side when I twisted and
let out the biggest cry. My stitch musta tore.

"Fo' real?" I say. "I got wounds."

Man, did I go to hurtin'.
DAMN!

Catch, he didn't care none.

"Don't sit high up and make truth about me," say Catch.
"If I hadn't had heat . . ." And he waved the gun large.
"You'd be rested cold in City Morgue right beside that
dumb-ass Ricky-Ricky. I fucking delivered you over
ten blocks and let your Mexican *brother* bust on me, so
I could get *your* life saved. Don't fucking make me
out heartless or coward or some bullshit. Everything I do
is about keepin' us all beating in our chest and outta the
ground."

I didn't have nuthin' to spit back.
I was outta thought.
And my side hurt complete.

"Shit," he say, holding out his hand. "I give you a lift."

"I don't need your lift," I say. "I got strength."

"Yeah . . . a'ight," he say. "I gotta make time then. Peace."

I rest there on that stoop.
Collecting what just went down.
Everything a clutter, backed-up traffic jam
in my thought. How did Catch and me get
to being so uneven not halfway through summer?
We ain't even put time on the Fourth yet.
Man . . . what was we doing?

Keeping eyes on him kicking it down the middle
of the street, I think how he don't look like the
guy I useta tell all my think to.
He look like one of 'em soldiers off to some war.
The way I seen guys in movies
enlist and leave what they know behind.

You couldn't a told me ever that Catch and me
have such distance when school let out.
I just wouldn't have believe on it.

I prop myself to my feet.
Hurtin' so fixed-fierce on every move.
It was a mad pain that shivered me
side-to-back and 'round again.

Three block and a half,
I drag past the elevator
that never climb with any kinda consistency.

By the time I hit the fourth floor, I was spent on the real.
No question.
I was done.

I come in the apartment and Monica was set
up on the couch ready to go toe-to-toe.

"I know you ready to dig," I say. "I just can't."

I turn the box fan jammed
in the window up on high.

"What happen?" she ask. "Your affect defeated."

"Just let me chill. Fo' a few. I give you truth.
I just need to stretch time."

And in what Tony might've called Divine Intervention,
Monica let me chill.

"We gonna have words," she say.

"I feel it," I answer.

She went off to her room.

I ease careful to the couch.
and stretch
b i g .
All the way flat.
Man, did 'em cushions feel good.

Kick off my sneaks and just settle solid when
upstairs, Juice Box's dog chew on something
with snarl and bark.
Man, did he have some volume.
Maybe he woulda been the best dog ever if
Juice Box didn't teach him how to hate.
Ain't no comin' back for a dog learn to hate.

Just when I thought I was setting a drift,
I hear this moan . . . deep, almost howl.
Crying and calling, "Jesus, I just can't take
no more of this senseless hurt. Jesus, please."

Mighty Mildred wail
in the apartment below.
She go on like she just done found out
Ricky-Ricky got flat-fixed.

Monica step outta her room.

"Where is you off?" I ask.

"Gonna go downstairs," she say. "Sit with her.
See if company give her some peace."

She grab her keys off the kitchen table.

"Theo," she say.

"Yeah?" I manage.

"Please, keep time inside," she say.

"I ain't movin'."

Monica made out the door.
Locking me in snug.
Mildred go to sobbing.
Man, it was the deepest pain I ever heard.
And I heard women cry on losing their children.
It ain't a sound unique to the Split.

But I dunno.
This . . . it was different.

Ricky-Ricky.
Flat-fixed fo' what?
Fo' trying to make cool?
Fo' being different?
Fo' thinkin' he had any kind of speak Money Mike
put ears to?
Shit!
It all set me so spun up with his grandma weeping.
I drop in my buds and play out some music
till I just

drift

o   u   t   .   .   .

When You Cook Up Truth

The snap-sizzle woke me up.
Monica was in the kitchen
cooking and saying her French
lesson from the CDs she been
bringing in all summer from the
public library.

Half my face marked up from
the couch pillow.
I'd dropped off deep.
TV news on silent.

Newswoman smile with her
perfect teeth. Smiling while

reporting on a plane crash in
India somewhere.
That's straight-up strange to me.
How newspeople do that all the time.
Especially on the 24-hour channel.
Bodies be dropping—people murdered
or sick—earthquakes and folks fighting
fo' land. Epic to their scale, hard shit,
and those newspeople keep sitting witness,
smiling.

I had to turn it loose.
It just too annoying.

I scoop up my phone.
It was twelve noon
and a handful of minutes
fo' real!
I'd been down four hours straight.

Whip out a text to Jimmy.
Tellin' him to ask Gabs to throw a reach
to Tisha's cousin Nia. I hate going it like that
to hold time with her, but I definitely wanna
step. Even if we just converse fo' a few.

I crippled off the couch, hand clutched
at my side like it was gonna keep
my sore parts from hurtin'.

Monica was solid on the French speak.

Sincerely.
But no matter how smooth she talk it,
it just hit my ear funny.

"Hey," I say.

She startled.

"Don't creep," she say.

"I walked tall," I say. "You just couldn't hear
me over all that French speak."

I look at the skillet with surprise.
Monica ain't usually what any of us call kitchen
skilled. She burn the toast fo' it hit the toaster.

Her phone went to popping.
She check through it faster than anyone I know.

"Quit loitering there, and fix you a plate," she say.

"Nah . . . I ain't hungry."

"Yes, you is. Don't lie at me. Your stomach a growl.
You just scared I'll kill you."

We was tense —
Then we just

laugh.

Laugh so hard
my side went hurting.

"A'ight, but you kill me, and Hilda gonna be fierce,"
I say.

I pile on some eggs, bacon, biscuits,
and home fries.
Give it all a sniff.
It smell on the even.

"Go on and sit it out," she say.

She fix herself up a plate and eased back in a
chair.

"You find any trouble last night?" she ask. "That
why you crippling more than yesterday?"

"Nah. No edge. Just sore. I kept my cool
through the evening."

"Why didn't you give ears when I ring?"

I get up and pour some sweet tea.

"Just got caught up," I say. "A lot just got going."

I come back to sit.
Take the first bit of 'em eggs and damn . . .
They was Denny's good!
Wow!

Home fries got seasoning on 'em.
Didn't even taste burnt.

"You lethal on this meal," I say.

She shifted in her seat.
Couldn't seem to find a way to settle in.

"Wooo, this baby need to step, Theo. I'm gonna
eat up half the block before it comes loose."

"You just ain't made for all that," I say.

"All what?"

"You know, babies. It ain't your default like
some of the girls 'round the Split."

"What you got to say about being unfit?" she ask.

"I ain't say you unfit. Say you ain't made for all . . .
this."

I put eyes back on my plate.

"You know I got respect," I say. "You could've
stopped that baby's heart down at the clinic.
I know you think on it hard, 'specially with Hilda
on you the way she was. But you made different.
You didn't make no easy way outta your mistake.
I just . . . you ain't gotta keep it. Nobody think on the
less."

She tighten up her lips and smile in that forced
way she do when she on the mad.

"This coming from Hilda?" she ask. "I know
she want me to turn this baby loose."

"Nah," I say.

"Something from Catch?"

"I got thoughts," I say. "They don't all belong
to someone else's think."

Yeah, she was mad.
Lean back in her chair.
Eyes deep on her plate.

That's when the keys start turning the lock.

Hilda blow in without a moment to pause.

"We gonna have time, right now," she say to me.
She pull out a chair at the table with us.

"He tired," say Monica, going back to her plate.

"Not too tired to stay out all night," say Hilda.
"Do you not feel it when I tell you to stay inside?
Am I speaking out gibberish?"

I just cross my arms and lean on back.

Wasn't nuthin' I could speak that would hold
space in her ears.

"You done gone fool," she say. "One hundred and
ninety-nine percent teenage boy fool," say Hilda.

Then she turn it on Monica, who was in no mood.

"You was supposed to have eyes on him."

"I only got two," Monica say.

"Then put that baby in your belly on watch and make
it four. I am wore out. Do y'all hear me? I am walking
in circles half the time because I ain't sleep when I do
get a moment to stretch."

She slam her fist on the table and shook it all up.

"Hey," say Monica.

"Don't you 'hey' me," say Hilda.

Monica push her plate to the side.
Hilda done come between a pregnant woman
and her meal.
Man, did I wanna step outta this one.

"Tony wouldn't shake a plate to make a point,"
Monica say.

"Tony ain't here to keep watch," say Hilda.

And she ain't never hold speak like Tony was ended.
Shit.
She always make like he with us every step.
Keepin' us safe.
Keepin' us right.
Keepin' us on together.

Hilda close those angry eyes.
She inhale deep.
Her stomach expand out wide.
It was all her work to retain some kinda cool.

"I'm serious on laying low, Theodore" say Hilda.
"And don't think I don't know you was at the church
last night."

I seen quick that Monica hadn't done me in on that
truth.

"Everyone I know buzzing about Ricky-Ricky dying,"
say Hilda. "And it's a terrible thing, Theodore. But
he wasn't yours to care for."

That's where she wrong.
That's where she ended it for me.

Ricky-Ricky been there.
Been there after Tony got snapped.
The guys didn't know what to say.
They was on about revenge and fighting only

we didn't know who to fight on.
Not fo' sure.
Part of me wanted to fight on somebody.
Mostly, I just wanted to cry it out in my pillow
when nobody hearing.

And yeah, Ricky-Ricky wasn't the kinda brother
you could hold real conversation with.
He scatter in his thought.
But he be the only one get how alone
I feel losing Tony.

"I'm serious about Houston," say Hilda. "I'm calling
your aunt later on when she off work."

"You can save your minutes 'cause I ain't
being shipped."

And I took my plate to the sink and strut.

"Hey," she say.

I kept walking.
Straight up into my room.
Door shut tight.
I'd actually turned back on Hilda A. Clark,
and she hadn't dropped fury across my ass.

The sky gonna open up and rain down hundred-
dollars bills fo' sure.

That's when —

Hilda bust through my door.
Come straight at me the way she done at the hospital.
Only this time she gripping Tony's belt.

"Hell, nah," I say. "You ain't whupping on me."

"Hilda," say Monica.

Hilda take a hold of my squirm
and strike me on my ass—my back.
Any damn where she could make that belt connect.

"Hilda, leave him!" say Monica. "He got hurt on him!"

"You gonna make ears for me," say Hilda. "You gonna
give me attention to the rules."

Only, I turn quick . . .

I . . .

I didn't mean

to turn

quick!

I ain't

n e v e r

e v e r

turn quick on my moms.

N E V E R .

Mike, 'fore he was Money,
he done what I just done.

Only he wasn't on to defending himself.
He mean to strike her.

The two of 'em come at each other hard.
Didn't matter Mike been her favorite of the three of us.
When Hilda got knowledge to Mike's full intent
to have me join the Jives,
that split
him
and
her
fo' good!

Hilda call on her biggest roar.
She on a burn like I ain't know—
couldn't know.
He was thug to her,
and ain't nobody use that word on the light
in our home.
Never!

She tell Mike
that he was the man of the family with Tony buried.
That he better quit acting the boy.

And that was all it took.

Mike slapped her red face.
And that shit finished fast 'cause
I ain't never felt a beast up in me so immediate.
I clench my palms to fist and beat on him.
Man, was I a wind-up-go.

Monica step between all us.

Mike just
laugh and
laugh
and

l a u g h .

That cultivate me to madder.
So I grabbed the kitchen knife, and he quit his laugh.

See, you can cuss Hilda if you brave, but you never
hit my moms red faced. I don't care who you is.

N   E   V   E   R   !

But when Hilda bust up in my room right then,
comin' at me with Tony's belt,

I just went automatic, you know? I

turn

   quick.

I hit my moms.
Hilda's eyes made me

s m a l l e r
than I ever be.

She take time 'fore she scoop herself up
from the wall she lean.
She take time 'fore she walk past Monica,
leaving the belt on the floor.
She take time 'fore she leave
on out my door.

Closing it still.

She was
d   o   n   e   .

Can't Hold Sleep

Jimmy be blowing up my phone all day Saturday
and into the night.
I got so over his texts and rings, I turn off
my phone.
Try to sleep and put loose from my mind
how it all went down with Hilda
earlier in the day.
She didn't say a single word to me.
Not at supper.
Not when she go to bed soon so she could
get up early fo' a side job she pick up cleaning.

Her leaving this morning is what stir me
outta sleep.

I take a seat out up on the fire escape,
keeping watch on Hilda make fo' the bus stop.
The sun
just start yawning, almost alert enough
to greet on the sky.

Wiggle Jones come singing praise and hallelujah
as he push his rusty ol' shopping cart
right down the middle of the street.
Cars go to giving him noise on their horns.
He laugh and sing louder.
His cart overflow with trash bags of cans.
The streamers he tie on be filthy.
They look as rugged
as he do.

Wiggle Jones was a longtime homeless brother.
He got a sister and two nieces live in the hood,
and they offer him stay.
Way I hear it, he say the walls crush his think.
He gotta be free to keep the energy up.
Guess that mean he can't bathe neither, 'cause
anyone get in distance to him know he got
funky-funk.

City bus hold stop down the block.
People on.
People off.
The hood was waking up fo' Sunday morning.

Tasty-Taste Doughnuts be baking
beast-good yum 'cross the street.

I was all on that fo' breakfast
when Monica put knock to my door.

"I'm perched," I say.

She step, come to the window.

"Couldn't sleep?" she ask.

"Nah . . . my head too full."

"Can I draw a seat?" she ask.

I chuckle.
As big she was, no way she getting out
on the fire escape.

"You might wanna wait on that?" I say.

She grin, shake her head.
"Punk," she say, "I ain't too big to make this
window."

And there Monica go.
Leg pushing, half-crawling.
It was the largest mess of moving I'd ever seen.
Her trying to negotiate that stomach with
the resta her.

"Close your laughing," she say.

"Yeah . . ." I grin. "I close it."

The sun had crashed over Bellwood Estates
or as we call it, the Projects.
Fifteen floors, fifteen doors per floor.
It was packed and spilling out.
Right then, though, the sun wrap the edges up.
It kinda glow.

"She say anything to you?" I ask Monica.

"Not a breath."

I adjust my sit.
Reach in my pocket and pop one of 'em pain pills.

"You being easy with those?" she ask.

"I couldn't be no easier. Trust on that. But I'm
ached."

Monica close her eyes for a few.
Breathe all deep.
She into that yoga meditation stuff.
I can't wrap my think on it, but it keep her right.

"I forget how different it all is before the day go,"
she say. "Even the trash look cleaner."

Up high, that early, the hood seem softer.
Maybe it help how the sun coming up blushing
the clouds and painting everything new.

"I know you didn't mean to hit her, T," Monica say.

"She know it too."

"I don't think she do," I say. "Hitting her wasn't direct in my think."

"I know that."

"I just needed some relief. Fo' her to slow her process. She was all up in her idea of me."

I put eyes on the street.

"She look at me like I was him," I say. "Like I was Mike."

"She stunned. And she wore thin."

"We all wore thin, Monica. You, me, people at the church, Mighty Mildred, Jimmy, Yo-Yo, and Catch."

She did not take to hearing Catch's name.

"My truth is clear," I say. "Everyone sliced thin. Hilda ain't the only one in struggle."

I love my moms.
Truth.
She hard, but in that way, she try to keep me safe.
Keep me straight.
Her need ain't unreasonable.
But she don't hear on my struggle.
All she see is how I do it all off.

Maybe I do different from how she do
but that don't mean it off.

"Here's the truth as I know it best, Theo," say Monica.
"Hilda have a lot to carry in this world. The two of us.
Tony being gone and Michael enlisted. Now, you know
Hilda and me don't lock ideas into a line every day. But,
I think she tryin' to do you right. And I know you aren't
Michael. You never been nothing like him. Even when
you almost join."

And that was the split in all of us
after Tony got flat-fixed.

Mike drop ink on my hand.
Telling me how I always be taken care of
and have a hundred brothers fo' life.
And we was brothers.
I wanted to believe his speak.
Even if I didn't trust on it complete.
But then I see how he do.
I see how he roll.
Pushin' li'l brothers nine, ten, eleven.
Shit.
Them kids oughtta be out breaking
backboards and chasing each other in the
park.
But Mike fillin' their heads with all that speak
he do on me.
Say to 'em how they daddies in lockdown,
and people gonna hurt on 'em 'less they enlist.

It was fucked up!

"What you thinking on?" Monica ask.

I shook my head.
I know I can hold speak with her,
but her and Mike was bonded.
They had this connect.
Almost a secret speak 'bout the world and books,
and how to make the perfect root-beer float.

I could never tell her what I suspect deep.
Money Mike had something to do with Tony's death.
He didn't pull the trigger, but I'm sure he was in on it.
'Cause Jives put Tony down.
I know 'cause I seen the ink on the shooter's hand.
And when I confront Mike, tell him I ain't enlist
with killers and slingers, he done what he had to do.
Beat me near death.
Show the Jives that blood wasn't love.
Jives Fo' Life!

"Stop it," she say.

"What?" I ask.

"Stop renting out space in your head to worry
on Michael."

"You brain-reading or something?"

"Theo, if that were on, I'd known to never share time

with Buffalo," she say. "You got this way of running
your hand over that ink when you think on Michael."

I hadn't ever even notice, but she right.
I did.

She wobble to her feet.

"I'm hungry for nine," she say. "How's you?"

"I could eat."

"Yeah? Well help me in, and I'll get us something
going."

Soon as she in the window and out to cook,
I ease on my bed and pop on my cell.

Trail of messages from Jimmy and Yo-Yo.
Not a word from Catch.
Jimmy sayin' people mobilizing.
They pumping signs all up in protest.
Demanding the City to change the tone of the street.
Make it safe fo' black people to hold speak with the po-lice.

Jimmy snap a video of the crowd and post it up.
They was over hundred people strong.
TV news out there too.

> People, chanting, "Black on black. We gotta
> quit that!"

But 'em people in Jimmy's video wasn't the real news.
I seen that quick when I get on the Net.
I click on this news link.
Someone drop matches off Strawberry Hill Lane
last night. Burn up Swanti's Nails and Taco's Tacos.

Now, setting stuff on fire, that make big news.
That got people's attention.
And it didn't make no kind of smart sense.
Raging on business places.
Nuthin' to gain fo' the hood torching up in that
part of town.
Nuthin' to gain fo' anyone else neither.
Them reporters were "speculating" 'cause

> "Black teenagers wearing hoodies
> were seen in the area earlier last night . . ."

And it wouldn't matter if black teens
be strutting hoodies all over the City.
There were "black teenagers," hoodies up,
near them burnt businesses at some point,
so, 'course, they must've done it.

That news made me crazy, so I just turn it
loose.
Kicking into my heat clothes,
white T-shirt and baggy ball shorts,
when my phone went to popping.

The text say:

At the Court. 10

The number come up unknown, but I knew
who be callin' me out.

Money Mike had found time fo' me.
That's the kind of time I just didn't
w   a   n   t   .

We Was Brothers

I ain't gonna lie. I was mad nervous to be
steppin' down to the Court knowing
Money Mike meeting me there.
I was sweatin' crazy wet.
Ain't even 10 on the morning, and the
air sticky-burn.

Streets be humming.
Protesters assembling by the Rec Center.
I seen them as I go on.
Lotta white kids up in there too.
I can't hate on 'em 'cause of their skin.
They tryin' to do right with the cause.
Can't hate on tryin' to make it right.

Jimmy been pumping message

through my cell like it got no limit.
He real chatty.
Wanted to connect.

But I didn't shout out to the guys
'bout meeting up with Money Mike.
They had too many bruises and breaks
to have to dig again.
And I couldn't be sure this was a dig,
but if it go like that, I ain't gettin' 'em
in the way of it.

Didn't tell Hilda or Monica neither.
I didn't tell nobody nuthin' 'cause
whatever speak Money Mike have fo' me
I wasn't gonna put no direct hurt on nobody else.

I just wanted all this to be
clear and ended.

I ain't no soldier.
I ain't want no battle.
I'd be easy to just call up Nia,
play ball with the guys, and
act like none of this ever went down.

Money Mike hated on me for not enlisting.
True.
But maybe we could make cool.

We was brothers by blood.
Seem like it oughtta hold time for something.

But fo' real, soon as I come 'round the corner
to the Court, I seen through the fence this
wasn't gonna be us makin' cool.

Money Mike pick me up in his sight straight quick.
Make step toward me with Brother Jive
from the bodega other night at his side.

Two Jives shoot hoop and keep me in their view.
They was rugged street soldiers.
Lockdown ink on their faces,
big shades and flame sneaks.
Wearing sweatshirts in the 90-degree heat.
Them fools straight down the middle insane.

Jay Ridge lean along the wall.
Dropping texts and holding eyes on the scene
at the same time.
And he was worked over harder.
Brother knew a lot of bruises.

"You ain't bring nobody?" ask Money Mike.

"This ain't nobody's cool," I say.

He kinda laugh.
I didn't see the funny.

"You a fucking Boy Scout," he say. "Shit, more
like Girl Scout."

Brother Jive crack a smirk.

I wanted to strike that shit up off his face.

"Your face sewed up crooked," Money Mike say.

He reach for me, and I push him back.

"You call me out to joke on my face?" I ask.

I straightened my back.
Held my stance.
Money Mike playing me like I was some
dead mouse in a stray's mouth.

I ain't fool.
I ain't flat-fixed.
And I sure ain't timeless.

"Look at you," he say. "Try to sell that rage.
Let me drop this on you. Playing hard ain't the same
as being hard, T."

"Why you call me out?" I ask.

"I needs to talk to you."

I held my quiet.
Feelin' the sweat chase down my back.

"Whatcha tell the po-lice?" he ask.

I shook out my head.

"What you think?" I say.

"I ain't playing you, T," he say. "You see
any gloves on my hands?"

Brother Jive step it closer.

Jay Ridge took notice.
Slipping his phone in his pocket.

"I ain't say nuthin' to the po-lice," I answer.

"He lying," say Brother Jive.

"Shut your face," I say to Brother Jive.

"Shut *my* face," say Brother Jive, reaching for
heat.

Money Mike hold up hands to him.

"Put that shit away," Money say. "We got eyes
and ears all over us."

Money Mike give his attention back my direction.

"A'ight, little brother. You ain't say nuthin'
to the po-lice."

He consider his thought with precision,
scratching the scruff of his chin.

"So, why they sniffing so big?" he ask.

"I dunno. Maybe 'cause you kill another kid.
Only Ricky-Ricky . . . he ain't like the others.
He never do harm or get high or challenge up.
Maybe him gettin' flat-fixed . . . maybe
that wear some people thin, and maybe *they* talking
to the po-lice. 'Cause you done him wrong
in hard daylight like you king—"

He threw me up against the chain fence.
My whole body went to hurting.
I swear!
Even my feet.

"I *am* the muthafucking king. You see anyone roll
the way I do in West Split? Huh?"

He jam his arm so deep up in my throat.
I couldn't breathe for nuthin'.
My throat seem like it gonna cave.

"Theo, I got Pigs asking questions all over.
I got squad Pigs cruising. Some of my guys dragged
in for questions. Only they ain't spit no answers.
'Cause they understand what it means to be a real
brother."

"Can't breathe, Mike."

He press up in my throat even harder.

My head ready to go light out.
I just knew it.

"News cameras and people up in protest shit.
And it's all 'cause you couldn't stay on your side
the hood."

Air.
I needed some . . .

"You giving me attention?" he ask.

"You ain't . . . king."

He punch me in the gut.
Then again.
Then across my face.

I drop back deep into that fence
gasping and hurtin'.

The stitch in my side broke.
Cut go to bleed.

I was
barely
  holding up.

My breath was loose.

"You coulda been a Jive," he say. "You coulda

had something, fool. Look at you in your pharmacy
baggy T-shirt. You ain't nuthin'."

Jay Ridge jog in.
I struggle to hold breath.

"He got the know," say Jay Ridge. "Let's walk this."

"Is that right?" Money Mike ask me.
"You got the know?"

I just hold there, clutching my side tight.

"Better listen to Hilda and make step to Texas," he say.
"'Cause I ain't doin' you no more favors."

I held on to that fence, mad sick to my stomach.
What he know 'bout what Hilda speaking at me?
What they negotiate without me in the know?

Hell, nah.
He ain't no king!

All he know 'bout was beatin' and shootin',
slingin' and intimidatin'.
That ain't how you raise nobody up.

My eyes kept time with him struttin' big off
the Court. Watching all them guys
roll off large, SUV-style.

Lord, truth?
I couldn't hold my step.

I clench the fence and sway 'fore I drop
to the ground.

That sky.
So bright, white-blue.
So sparked.

Part of me wanted to lay there till I couldn't
lay no more.
Till the gospel song from Sunday church I
be hearing come carry me right up to Tony,
sittin' up somewhere on one of 'em
puffed-up clouds.

Sittin' between the earth and sun maybe.
Eatin' one of 'em big ol' bowls a spaghetti he
like to stir up every Friday night.

Spaghetti
swimming in meaty red sauce. Covered
in that fresh parmesan cheese he grate
up by the bowl.
He dig on that meal to such heights.

All us family sit at the table.
In speak on how our day go or what we wanna
watch on TV
Hilda so full of her life then.
She only on one job, and she didn't hate on it.

And man, did Tony love on my moms.
He appreciate on her.
And that just make her light up.
He was the smoothest, coolest, smart-thinking
brother in the City.

Just thinkin' on him swell up my eyes
with water.
Make me wanna bawl 'cause when I put look
to the side,
I see Tony like he next to me on the real.
Like in Trejo's car when we frenzy to the hospital.

I see Tony
lying on the floor of that Quick & Grab Grocery
with a loaf of bread still in his hand.

His glow just

f   l   o   a   t   .   .   .

And me shaking beside him.
Not knowing what to speak
seeing him fade.
Seeing all that
b   l   o   o   d
and
pissing myself warm
knowing he gone
and
I was next.

And when I look up,

I see the Smoker pointed
straight at me.
I see the Jive ink on the guy's hand.
His eyes zombie-dead,
pointing that heat
right to the middle of my loud thoughts.
They be
   s c r e a m i n g
inside!

Lookin' direct into my end,
really seeing it on the arrive,
made everything

quiet.

It made it
fastandslow . . .
slow   and   fast—
and
that fat woman Tony try to calm
kept screaming.

People
talking in tongues. And
some part of me . . .

just
      let
          go.

'Cause I didn't have no heat in my hand. I
didn't have no one to make it stop. Tony
done faded out
holding a loaf of bread.

And 'em eyes lookin' at me with that
Smoker . . .
they was dead and cold and didn't feel
nuthin' fo' me or any us there.

I shut my eyes tight.

I calls out to Hilda and Monica
in my mind.
Tells 'em I love 'em
and
ask God to keep watch on both 'em
and the guys.

And then I hear one voice through all
the carrying on up in there.

"Stop! Not him."

And that maxed brother who say it
look at me . . .
he spare me outta my death.

And shot the register guy.

Tony . . . he —

I'd pissed myself.

That fat woman . . . she still screaming.

And Tony—

"Young Black," Smokey say to me.

I'd drifted in my think.
So drifted I didn't see any those people
take to gather 'round me on the Court.
Lookin' on me.

"Speak it if you got time," say Smokey.

He kneel to my side.

"What is you?" I ask.

"What is me?" say Smokey, putting attention
under my shirt. "A bear. Just like you."

Smokey dressed button shirt to tie.
They all dress nice.
Like they come from a funeral.

"Am I dead?" I ask.

"Who is you?" ask Smokey. "Do you know?"

My side was wet with blood.

"Shit," I say. "I got red, Smokey."

"All right," say Smokey. "Let's help this."

And this brother, fo' real, lift me straight up
like I was a baby just born out.
Carry me to his car and sit me low in the backseat.

"Your nice shirt," I say. "It's wet."

Smokey say, "Hang steady, Young Black.
We get you all set."

And seriously, I don't know much next.

It was so hot.
So tired.
 Hungry.
  Hurtin'.

I close my eyes and imagine Tony
and
that bowl of spaghetti
and
his smile.

My pops . . .
he had a way to

g l o w .

Smokey the Man, Yo

There's a fly buzzing up in Smokey's
apartment.
He don't offer it no time.
He got a needle and thread and ready
to stitch my side complete.

"You sure on this?" I say.

"You just lost a stitch or two. I'm always good
for a stitch . . . or two. I work medical in the army."

"You a man nurse or something?"

"Or something," he say, slipping that needle direct.

"You sure?" I ask. "'Cause that hurt a brother."

That needle got me panting.

He focus eyes on my side.
Grinning, he say, "I'm sure you need to keep away
from your brother. Now, just breathe, Young Black.
This will go quick."

Seeing my skin catch thread made me
wanna spit up everything I have for breakfast
and wanted fo' lunch.

"He text me," I say. "He wanna have speak."

"Looks like," Smokey say, "he wanna agitate you.
Draw you out."

"He just try to scare me—OUCH!" I say.
"You almost complete?"

"Breathe, Young Black. Just breathe. And maybe,
this is just me in thought, but your brother's motives
feel ulterior. I don't trust on his eyes."

Smokey snap the thread precise.
He done.
Smokey wash off my side.
Damn, did that cool rag feel good.

"This is some cut you earn," say Smokey.
"It's gonna scar for sure."

Smokey hold out the inside of his arm.

Stretched from wrist to elbow run this
big-ass, deep scar.
It was seriously raise up on his skin.

"Who cut you up?" I ask.

Smokey hold watch on it.
Chuckling to himself.

"When you a soldier, you sometimes acquire scars.
Some on the outside . . . like this big old thing. Some
on the inside. Those are probably the worst
'cause ain't nobody see them 'cept you."

Smokey throw away the needle and bloody
gauze.

"But they become these stories you tell," he say.
"So you know you survived."

"I guess I'll have a story then."

"That's the thing," he say. "You ain't a soldier.
You ain't supposed to have these stories."

"Smokey, I didn't look to dig. At least, that's not
why I step. But Money push up on me—he *wanted* me to dig."

Smokey nod. "That's when you walk."
I half-chuckle.
Smokey was a spark brother, but he off.

"You are not a soldier," Smokey say.

"Nah, but people looking," I say. "People wanting
change. You seen how they go up in that church
when we hold speak. They on about rising."

"Violence is not that change." And he serious
in this word. "Violence is not our answer."

"I feel to that," I say. "It just ain't that clean
in its delivery. I don't wanna do no battle, but
sometimes people just battle up on you.
You gots to battle back. That's the play."

"This ain't some game," say Smokey. "There is no play.
See, when people drop, they go."

I was stirred.
He hold speak like I was li'l in my think.
I know what it mean to see someone fade.
I seen.
I got eyes.
I watch too many lights fade.
But I don't carry heat.
Don't sling.

"Hey," he say. "Where is you in there?"

I took stance.
Sorta.
More like wobbled.

"You think I don't know," I say. "That flat-fixed
is real. I seen Ricky-Ricky and more than him.
You ain't that far outta touch in your experience
to not know I had to make step—*speak* my truth
to Money Mike when he call me out today."

"Then you done with all that then, right?" ask Smokey.

I held unsteady.
One hand to my side, the other on the back of the chair.
I was sweating mad.

"Sit yourself, Young Black," say Smokey. "You
aren't full to your potential just yet. Hold
some time in the chair."

He gather up all the first aid stuff and
put steps to the kitchen.
Which ain't like our place.
It's a whole separate room.

My phone go to popping.
Jimmy dropping text.
Asking what went down at the Court.
Say people be dropping
speak on it. It was on everyone's know.
I tell him I'll be quick to explain.
He didn't struggle with me about the delay.
Just wanted to know what was up.
Know that people was in a march down the streets.
They rised up even harder than the night
'fore.

I take a li'l time to speculate on Smokey's
walls. Family photos. Ol' school black-and-white
pics like when my grams was still drawing breath.
Pic of him enlisted.
Military-style.
Kid pic of who I think him.
Damn . . . he a thick-armed brother back when he li'l.

There he stand tall in one 'em.
Married up to a sweet, smooth, fox-cinch.
Ooooooh . . . she is something to be jealous on.
I make sore steps to get better focus on 'em.
Wow . . .
They both aglow.

Smokey drop steps from the kitchen.
He holding a tray with drinks.

"Who she?" I ask.

Smokey make on that cool-brother grin.

"Come sit your pain down," he say.

I take it to the couch. Stretch careful and slow.
That pain chew my side up deep.

"That beautiful angel was Dallas Lynette Morgan."
Smokey kept with his grin, but it ain't hold
right. It was like he making his face go
where it don't want.

"Her time got met before we could live that
joy together," he say.

"How she go out?" I say.

"Put this down."

He hold out a drink he make.
Just to be fo' real, the mix didn't soothe
my interest.
It was soldier green and bubbly.
It
smell like feet
and
lemons
and
onions
and
something I couldn't know.

"That's raw, man," I say.

"My mama, God give her blessings, she
make that for me after the first time I got shot."

"You been pierced?" I ask.

He hold up his hand.
His fingers make out four.

"Damn . . ." I say. "Someone intent to chill you
permanent."

He chuckle.

"Yes, Young Black. There have been some people
who have wanted to bury me one time . . . maybe two."

I put eyes back on that photo of him and Dallas.

"You think on her?" I ask.

"All the time," he say.

"Yeah . . ." I say.

"Put taste to that drink before it go off," he tell me.

"Smokey, I gotta be truth. I think this is done off."

He laugh.
Damn, he go to roar in his laugh.
He was a bear.

"Yeah, I think that too when my mama gave it
to me," he say. "Still had to give it my time."

So I close my eyes and yucked my face.
Took in that deep breath like when you
jump in the deep end of City Pool.
And—

    WHAT THE HELL!
N A H !

It burn
and
I
cough
and my face go
ugly!

"Keep on," he say. "Halfway to the end of the earth."

And some way it went down.

"Nah," I say.

Shook my head trying to get the feel off me.

"You done my good mama proud," he say.

That drink 'bout climbed right back up.

"Breathe, Young Black. Isn't anything in that
remedy that will end you."

Then a knock come to the door.
Smokey didn't have it full open when Hilda
demand room to step.
She on fire.

"What I tell you, Theodore Todd Clark?" say Hilda.
"Is my speak too fast?"

Monica pick a slower pace but was there.

"Hilda . . ." say Smokey. "The boy's clean.
He wasn't lookin' for edge."

"Ronald Love, I don't need you to be defense
and judge," she say.

Ronald Love? What kind of name was that for a bear?

"Mama," say Monica.

"I let you come along, Monica, but this ain't your cool."
Then Hilda turn back to Smokey. "I appreciate the stitch. I
know you drop a solid needle. But my son know his days
are numbered in this hood. And those numbers come
faster if he leave my home."

"It's summertime, Hilda," say Smokey. "Young Black
needs to be out. People respect his act. He inspire them."

And that when she get direct in his face.
Don't think he didn't tower her.
Don't think she didn't care.

"Listen," she say. "You trying to rise people up. I
appreciate. I do. But he isn't gonna be some symbol
for the Jives to hate on no more. After the Fourth,
he's taking the train to Houston. Until then, he
ain't makin' time outta his room."

"What?" I say. "Hell, nah. You ain't shipping me."

"Don't you spit!" say Hilda. "We already got
deep uneasy between you and me."

"You ain't—"

"Clark Family," say Smokey. "Let's all be cool."

And believe this truth.
Hilda actually held her words tight.
That was a near first.
Smokey was the man, yo.

"The heat been high," say Smokey. "Weatherman
say we gonna break one-oh-five today. Now, that will cook
a thought before it get to cracking."

He make me funny in his think.
I just laugh.
Monica too.

"Hilda, you know I respect you, and your way
to raise any child under your roof," say Smokey.

"I ain't being shipped," I say.

"Young Black," say Smokey. "Let's be cool.
Can we hold our concern for the moment?"

I dip him a nod.

"All right," he say. "Now, here's how I'm seeing it. Let

me drive you all home. Then I'll make a trip to
Alman's Grocery. Come back and fix you all a meal
so you can gather your thoughts with a full stomach.
Cool your truth and be easy to one another."

I wasn't mad at a meal.
So long it don't hold flavor like that drink he up and
make me pursue.

Smokey work his eyes to us.
See if anyone go claim up his offer.

"I could be down with that," Monica say.

"I'm on it," I say.

"Hilda?" ask Smokey.

"Gather your step off that couch," Hilda say.

I struggle to make stance.
Come up to Hilda.

"'Bout what went down," I say.

"I got no time for your speak," she say. "I just can't
hang on all that right now."

We all made to the door
'cept Smokey.
Smokey held his step, waiting on Hilda to confirm.

"I ain't bend the time to eat all day," she say. "So I wouldn't be smart to oppose."

And Smokey go to that smooth brother grin.

"So it be, Clark Family," say Smokey. "So it be."

That's all it took
fo'
all us walk out

t o g e t h e r .

Drive-By

Monday Hilda made fo' work and
Monica gone fo' a checkup.
She ready to pop that baby
out!
She done past the calendar due.

I eatin' up leftovers from the meal Smokey
cook us when Yo-Yo go to ringing
my phone.

He say there was a drive-by on 15th and Vine.
Say DJ Spin got smoked. Want me to hit the
streets to check it.

I express how he don't appreciate my

situation. Hilda sincere on her speak
'bout putting me off to Houston.

But he plead on me.
Sayin' Catch acting off, and I need to be on
to collecting time with him.
Say Pinky go at Catch even worse
than we all bear the witness.

Don't get me wrong.
I ain't down with disrespecting my moms.
Fo' sure.
But Catch and me,
despite how we in disagree,
he still my best friend.

● ● ●

DJ Spin's mom was a hollering.
Her lungs were full of noise.
I hear her 'fore I get to her street.

The summer had been
hot with sweat and bullets.
But a drop in the daytime?
That didn't add.

Catch didn't throw me much time
as I come up.

"Your face look on," say Yo-Yo.

He knuckle-bump, drop-snap to me.

"Man, it still feel off," I say.

"I hear that," he say.

Some of the neighbors try to give
Spin's mom relief.
She wasn't having it.
Crying and screaming and holding on to him.
But he faded.

"How long he been laying out?" I ask.

"At least twenty minutes," say Yo-Yo. "We
can't be exact, but that's when we heard the
spray."

Bullets like raindrops.
It just happens in West Split.

"Cops?" I ask.

Catch laugh. "As usual, Pigs running on Pig
Time. We calling numbers on how long till they
show. You want in?"

"Nah, that's cool," I say.

I wasn't feelin' the whole
bet on a dead brother. That
just be off.

But Catch like to run numbers 'cause he good at 'em.
He couldn't spell the word *travesty*,
but he could tell you which numbers would lead to one.

And he clowns. It's how he makes his time
stretch when we in school.
How he distract other kids from him not
knowing how to make letters work together.

But give him a number, and he one
of 'em Wall Street smarts brother.
He can bend a number and make it ache
the way Jimmy do with girls.

No
DOUBT!

Now that Catch workin' for Nacho,
carrying heat on his back and rage in his soul,
I just don't know.

"What?" Catch ask me.

"How your face get more puffed?" I ask.

He just shrug.

"You know how it is," he say. "I ain't down
on it."

Yo-Yo right.

Catch real off.
Catch I grew up with was fading fast.
Who was this brother standing next to me?

Jimmy step up to us.
He was short on his breath.
Still wearing his Chicken Shack uniform.

"Damn, it is hot crazy, yo," say Jimmy.

"Why you heavy in your breath?" I ask.

"Tiny Lewis drop text. Say you guys were
watching bullets. I put speed to my step 'cause
ain't *none* you fools answer calls. Thought the
Jives might be bringing battle."

"Shit," say Catch. "Tiny Lewis got more bad eyes
than both my blind grandmothers. We ain't see nuthin'
spray. We come after."

"What happened?" ask Jimmy.

Man, did Jimmy smell deep-fried.
Brother need a shower and deodorant in the
worst absolute way.

"Yo-Yo and me heading to the Court when we
hear the bullets bust out," say Catch. "We got bets
going on how long it take the po-lice to
show."

"Y'all running numbers on a dead brother?"
ask Jimmy.

"I ain't in it," I say.

"We ain't running numbers on him. He dead,"
say Catch. "His number done. I'm just scoring
on how much time it take for the Pigs to show."

Right then, the cops roll up.

"Twenty-five minutes," say Catch. "Hell's yeah.
Pay up, fool."

Yo-Yo bust out five bucks.

Cops had shown up twenty-five minutes
after Spin's mom call 'em.
That was rich, man.
Like her street was edge no doubt.
Crackheads and trick turners were all
over the corners and doorways.
They was like decoration.
You just kinda knew they'd be there.
Still. People live up in here.
People like DJ Spin's mom.
And 'em Pigs show up on Pig Time.
Not like on TV or how they
frenzy to the crime up in South Pear.
Shit.
In South Pear, Pigs stop traffic on the real
to let people cross the street.

Cross the street!
That just never gonna happen in West Split.

Never.

And DJ Spin
been laying cold in his mom's front yard
in all this heat and all that time
she weeping and weeping.
Her nightgown cover wet in Spin's blood.

If you'd just come up like Jimmy had or the
po-lice, you'd think she got shot too.

The po-lice was trying to handle her.
Take DJ from her arms.
She was hysteric.
Wasn't onto none of 'em.
Cussing and a crying.
She was on the blame for their delay.

"Trejo came through blasting," Catch say.

I drop eyes to him immediate.
He keep looking over at DJ Spin's.

"That's what people saying, T," say Yo-Yo.

"For real?" ask Jimmy.

"It don't add," I say. "Trejo ain't got no reason
to ice Spin."

"I know he's your Mexican *brother,* but he still—"
say Catch.

"Why you always gotta ride?" I ask.

"Guys—" say Jimmy.

"Nah, I'm serious," I say. "You push me down at
my stoop 'cause I standing too tall for you. And
bite at me for not cutting Trejo loose 'cause you
two fought over Gabs back in another day?"

Catch chest pushed out.
He wanted to hit me.
That much was truth.

"You think you so evolved 'cause your daddy rub
time in South Pear," say Catch.

"You wack!" I say.

"You won't make easy with a Jive, but you got all
kinda time for a guy enlisted in the Skins," Catch say.

And I gotta be real.
I didn't have nuthin' to respond.
'Cause maybe, maybe he was right.

One thing was straight fo' me.
Catch could say 'lot about how Trejo roll these days.
But a broad-ass, daylight drive-by?

That just wasn't how he tagged.

And 'fore we could get any more heated to
each other, one of 'em squad car po-lice step to us.

"Be cool," say Jimmy.

"Hey, guys. I'm Officer Cross. Did you see
what happened across the street?"

"Nah, man," say Catch.

The cop dropped a look to each of us.

"You were standing here when we arrived," say the cop.

"So was they," Catch say, pointing to the crowd
gathering. "You ask them if they seen something.
Nah, you come straight to us four black men."

Catch was giving that cop hard eyes.

"Look, don't give me attitude," say the po-lice.

"Or what?" challenge Catch. "You gonna
Ferguson us?"

I knew Catch was carrying heat.
This was no good time to push the po-lice.
There is never a good time to push the po-lice
when you black.

"Sir, we didn't see nothing," Jimmy say. "They was just walkin' to the Court and heard the spray."

"It's truth," I say. "We all come to put eyes on what went down and see DJ's mama cryin', so we just hang. Outta respect."

The cop kept his suspicious high.
His hand near his gun.

"Did you know him?" he ask.

"Everybody know DJ," I say. "He spin records all over West Split. Drop needles in South Pear too."

The cop didn't follow.

"He's a DJ," I say. "Vinyl, man.
Scratch it ol' and new school."

Cop reach fo' his pad of paper.
Pen ready to go inking.

"Okay. I need to get your names," say the cop.

Catch didn't hesitate.
He speak with absolute certainty.
Almost like he wanted to be had fo' something.

"I'm Willy Robert," say Catch. "This scrawny brother with the cast up on his arm is James Marshall."

"Scrawny," say Jimmy.

"Duncan McGriff be this tubby fool and . . .
who is you?" Catch say to me.

Why was he diggin? I
wasn't in no mood,
but he . . .
he was intent.

"Theodore. Theodore Todd Clark, sir," I say to the
cop.

Catch grin. Shake his head.

The cop handed over his notepad.

"List your phone numbers next to your name."

Of course, we all put made-up numbers there
and hand it back to him.

As the cop step off, Catch say, "Don't forget to ask
all those other people what they see. Get their
names and numbers too."

"Be cool," say Jimmy.

"Whatever," Catch say to Jimmy. "He ain't gonna drop
me with all those newspeople setting up over there."

"Maybe he wasn't looking to drop nobody," I say.

"Pig show up twenty-five minutes after DJ drop,"
say Catch. "You gonna tell me he really care on
what happened? You more fool every day."

"Cool it," say Jimmy. "Quit eating on all this heat
between you."

"I ain't timeless, Catch," I say.

"You timed out," he say.

And I make move to jump him
and Jimmy
and Yo-Yo
split us
quick!

"Fucking po-lice across the street," say Jimmy.
"You both outta your cool sense? Now, keep it true.
We friends. A'ight?"

I hold my head back.
Catch did too.
And damn if he couldn't look tougher than me
any day.

We was settling out our heat when
bass blasts curl 'round the corner.
Gabs roll up in some new-ass ride.
'Em wheels make our distract ignite.

"Wow . . ." say Yo-Yo.

And it was wow fo' sure.
The hubs' chrome blinding.
Reflect red, glitter sparkly body.
Custom cut lines.

That shit was hot wheels.
Ain't no way it legit.

Tisha rode up shotgun,
and Nia
she hold down the back.
They make big with the top
down!

I ain't gonna lie.
Nia had my attention instant.
She putting eyes to me too.

That car deliver 'em right up to us.

"Y'all look tired," say Gabs.

"This heat spend a brother," say Catch,
giving me look.

Gabs just ignore Catch. They had history,
obviously,
and I think it was all she could do
not to have one of her
three brothers not doin' time drop him.

"Who inched over there?" ask Tisha.

"DJ Spin," say Yo-Yo.

Yo-Yo smile big at Tisha.
Brother ain't never gonna learn.
He ain't her crave.
Besides, he got chocolate in the corner his mouth.

"Damn . . ." say Tisha. "What a waste.
He was smack-crackle-pop fine."

Jimmy lean over the car. "Where you open this ride?"

"My brother had it dropped," say Gabs. "Ain't it fire?"

Jimmy was strained, no doubt.

"It's legit, James," Gabs say to him. "Easy."

She was
l y i n g . . .
and us guys knew it!

"You check the trunk?" ask Catch. "Might have
someone flat-fixed up in there."

Only reason Gabs didn't have Catch
dropped was 'cause they was a big,
special thing once
and no matter what she say, and she say
enough to wear a brother's ear to bleed,
she still carrying flame for him.
I could see it in how he just burns her.

"Anyways," say Gabs. "We gonna roll to the mall.
Get our consume on with air condition."

I couldn't take my stare off Nia.
She sweatin' me good with resistance.

Jimmy push off the car. "We gonna hang back."

"Oh, c'mon, baby," say Gabs. "Let's get some time
outta the Split. I'll buy you something flash."

"No," Jimmy say. "I don't need it."

Damn!

We all look at Jimmy.
He wasn't a guy to spit too hard
and definitely not at Gabs.
I mean, shit. She fierce.

"A'ight . . ." say Gabs. "You don't gotta be
so vocal in your feel. It's good."

And she actually seem hurt over the whole speak.

"I'm gonna stroll a bit," say Nia.

Tisha and Gabs was like "what?"

"Y'all burn it up in the mall," Nia say,
climbing out the car.

I offered to help her, but she wasn't havin' it.

"I got balance," she say to me.

"A'ight . . ." I say.

Gabs dropped the wheels on outta there.

Nia stood back to all us guys.
Watching the cops dance around DJ Spin.
Yellow tape strung.
Snapping photos and asking questions.

"You all know him?" she ask.

"He drop needle at most of Nacho's parties," I
say.

"But did you know him?" She turn to us.

I struck off the way she look.
Nuthin' about it was foolin'.
199 percent on the real.
Serious.

"Nah," I say. "Not the way we know each other."

She nod.

"That's too bad," she say.

Nia put eyes back to DJ's place.

"His mama gonna break, it look like."

Most girls in West Split act on like Gabs or Tisha do.
Well, most girls I meet up with.
Nia . . . she really stop the time. I

liked that.

"Brother shoot too much juice in his arm," say Catch.
"Run his tab too high. Or shacking too long with one
of Nacho's corner girls."

"What do you know about this?" Jimmy ask Catch.

Catch chuckle. "Nuthin'. I'm just making thought."

Me and Jimmy give him attention.

Catch
  made me uneasy.

With him diggin' at me.
Every day he act on a li'l more like Money Mike
and a li'l less Catch.
And havin' Pinky crack his back and try
break his spirit . . .
it just kill me inside out.

But not enough to have him roll up all
over me like I was half-fool.

That just ain't my cool.

And he was feelin' on it from the way
we give each other dark looks.

"C'mon, y'all," say Catch to all us.

He start walking, and we all follow.

"I'm just playing detective and shit," Catch say.
"I don't know why Spin get spent.
Ease y'all's look."

Yo-Yo kinda laughed.
Pull out that Duncan from his pocket
and went to tricking it.

"I shoulda snapped a pic of y'all's faces," say
Catch. "Hell, I still can."

He reach for his phone and annoy all us
'cept Nia, who kinda smile at us blocking his
snap.

"Whatever," say Jimmy. "Now you being a
punk."

Catch quit with the pic.

"Y'all really think I in on it," Catch say. "Spin
was my one solid to get my spit outside the hood.
That's flat-fixed now."

We come up where people on with protest.

"This is immediate," Nia say.

Catch kinda laugh. "Ain't gonna change nuthin'.
People be fool to think peaceful protest gonna
shift the mood."

We all held our watch and quiet fo' a moment.

"I'm gonna make time for the Court," say Catch.
"Who's with it?"

Jimmy lean in on me and Nia, "Why don't y'all grab
some pizza or something cool? We'll roll to the Court."

He slap-snapped me a shake and produced that
Jimmy cool-brother grin.

I felt my cheeks go hot just knowing what he
was grinning on.

The guys cut out.
Catch give me attention fo' a sec before they all
vanish on the other side of the crowd.

Nia and me, we stroll awhile.
Not really holding speak.
Just movin' through the hood.

"So . . ." she say.

"Yeah . . ." I say. "So, you been crossing my think."

"Is that your step?" she ask.

Damn, she crush a brother's start
'fore he know he get to go.

"Why don't you give me relief?" I ask.

I move a li'l close.
Closer than I used to doin' 'cause I talk a big game.
No doubt.
But girls I really feel somethin' fo' . . .
they make my courage shake.

"It don't cost you nuthin'," I say, "to give me relief."

"My time. And that's expensive."

We step on a bit.
She workin' that smile.
Those eyes.
Her hips put me in the mood.

"Can I step real?" I ask.

"So long you intent."

"What else you expect?" I ask.

"Brothers step to me all the time. Half-grab my breasts
with their look before they get to their speak."

"Really?" I ask.

"You didn't notice them?" she ask back.

"Can't not notice 'em. They just out riding, but it ain't my focus if that's the trip."

We cross over into the park.
Graffiti spray big up on the brick.

"See that one," I say. "That's Yo-Yo's."

"Your friend with the toy?" she ask.

"Yeah . . ." I say. "You should've seen us try to steady his weight on the ladder we borrow.
Said he had to get up high. Wanted the spray to hold time as long as it could."

"Can I ask you something?" she say.

I give her nod.

"Now, I ain't crushing your look, but seriously.
Why you always wearing a hood? Brother, we in a heat wave."

"It's lightweight," I say. "I cut the sleeves.
'Sides, it make a statement."

She laugh. "Seem a way to incite the police.
Make 'em quick to decide you suspicious."

I shook my head, just grinning.

"Speak it," she encourage.

"A'ight," I say. "Brother in a hoodie ain't
suspicious. Not all the time anyway. Me and the
guys . . . when Trayvon news broke, how he get no
justice, we all throw up hoods. Right off the
minute it went truth. Go down to the Court. Meet
up with these hipster kids that run the Rec Center.
They got their hoods up too. And Catch, he don't
like those hipsters, but they's cool. They didn't dig
on Trayvon getting no justice."

"True that," she say.

"It was a hot day, yo," I say. "I mean, blazing. We
carry 'round those gallon jugs of water. Went down
to Strawberry Hill. People call it where the hood
and the good cross. Stood out there with our backs
to the street, hoods all up and cars whipping by.
People shout things. Throw things. We didn't shout
nuthin' back. We didn't break or burn nuthin'. We
just stood."

"So you're an activist."

"Activist?" I say.

It never hit direct like that.
An activist.
Huh.

At the time, I just saw it as a way to keep
us all from gettin' pinched for something real
deep
like 'em brothers setting fire to shit.
Looting and raising hell from their angry hearts.

Activist.
That was tight.

"Yeah," I say. "Guess I was."

"You still are," she say. "Way you stand up for
that kid. Ricky? People are inspired."

"What you know about inspire?" I ask. "Awww . . .
you been thinking on me. Admit it. Yeah . . . you got
ears to be knowing about me."

She blush.
Damn, she a sweet shade of pretty.
It just weak me to the back of my knees.

"Maybe . . ." she say, "I think a little."

"C'mon. You be thinking on me. Thinking about
my grin. How I walk big."

I bust out in front.
Walk large and over-exaggerate my step.
She giggle.
I laugh.
We was in it.

The moment.
Just being like kids or something.

Then my side go to hurting.
My balance went loose.
It slow me for a moment.

"You got pain?" she ask.

"It's that cut I earn fo' being inspiring."

We took seat on the merry-go-round.
I throw one of 'em pain pills back.
She got eyes on the ritual.

"It's legit," I say. "I don't soar on
drugs fo' real time."

She put eyes to the kids in the park.
They was a lotta 'em.
Li'l black kids runnin' all 'round
with
li'l white kids
and brown kids.
Even a baby Asian kid chillin' in the sandbox.

No gangs.
No drugs.
No guns.
No hate.
They ain't learn it yet.

Just being kids.

"You think you'll leave West Split?" Nia ask.

"I'm fifteen."

Her mouth go to open wide.

"What?" she say. "I sure you was at least sixteen."

I adjust in my sit.
Straighten out my hoodie.

"Give me a few months. I'll be there."

"Fifteen . . ." she say.

She go to smiling.
Man, could she set the world in motion
with that expression.
Fo' real.
Serious!

"But yeah, to what you ask," I say. "I'm outta
here in two years. I been thinking on college
maybe. My sister, Monica, she always been on
'bout college. I wouldn't give it to her to know,
but I respect her more than almost anybody.
When she tell me she pregnant, I knew if anyone
could figure out how to keep a dream warm, it
would be her. She know what time it is, you know?"

We push with our feet.
Get that merry-go-round to go a li'l.
It move slow and that was fine.
We just keep to our going.
Push on past a needle in the dirt.
It was as calm as I'd been since everything
go down with Ricky-Ricky.

"Jimmy told Gabs your mom wants you to leave.
Because she thinks you're marked."

"Yeah . . ." I say.

"Does that scare you?"

I step to my feet—run-push.
Trying to make my think leave
the pain up in my side.

I
jump up
and
r i d e .

A sticky breeze coat us.
Nia keep eyes on me.

"It take too much time to be scared of a bullet or a
beating," I say. "I'd forget to breathe if I think on that
as much as I could."

We slow down.

"Trying to help Ricky-Ricky, it's not just what my
pops would've done," I say. "I mean, I useta share time
with that kid—with his grandma. They good solid
people. Shit. You probably think me a soft fool."

"Compassion don't make a man fool," she say.
"My dad, he got sent up for life when I was less
than a year. I grow up knowing him for a while on
weekend visits. But then we just quit going."

We come stopped and just settle.

"My mom started dating a decent brother with a lot of
compassion," Nia say. "I seen her light up for the first
time. I don't think my dad ever have compassion
for her . . . maybe anybody. The times I see him, he'd talk
on what he didn't have or what he shoulda have, but
he didn't want it honest."

"How he get locked down?" I ask.

"He pick up a Smoker. Killed two women and a man
during a robbery. Life times three."

"Damn, that's on," I say.

"Ain't it?"

She got up and started pushing us.

She got some strength in her run.
She jump on and man, she alive in her joy.

"Can I ask you?" I say. "You miss him?"

"Not too real. Why your face got length?" she ask.

"I miss my father *every day*. He kept us in good
clothes and full up in the belly. We weren't living
high-cash or nuthin'. But we did a'ight."

She sit up closer to me.
Her investment clear.

"Everybody in West Split respect him," I say.
"He always helpin' kids. Starting up teams on the Court
weekends. He bring people together, you know?"

"Can I know?" she ask. "How he go?"

I drag my sneak and bring us stopped.
I hadn't talked 'bout it to the detail very much.
Told the po-lice what I knew.
Even told Mike.
Way he act made me think he mixed in it.
Hilda didn't wanna know it all.
Monica only in parts.

But there Nia was.
In all the ways she make me intense, she
make me soft too.

"It was just getting on to cold. Tony and me, that's my
pops, we was done playin' ball at the Court. I could . . .
smell these tamales from the Mexican food place.
They only make 'em on Saturdays, you know? But
he was on 'bout getting home, so we rush it. Get and
go, you feel me? Yeah, so . . ."

Sitting there with Nia,
I could smell the crisp-cold air from that day.

The cold sweat from all that ball we play.

"So, me and Tony cut up into this li'l store real quick.
Hilda was on about milk and bread and some other
particulars. I can't remember in full."

Tony, he was joking me.
We laugh like it were going out of trend.

"These guys come runnin' in the store.
They got Smokers. They all maxed up, you know?
Tony didn't try to be no hero. Just try to calm
this woman over by the candy. I mean, she was
losin' it. And it made one of 'em guys fit to cap her.
And Tony only attempt clarify to that brother that
she scared, you know? And that brother
just dropped him,
    hard.
Not a second thought."

I shook my head.

It was all too much, but I couldn't
let it set up stage on me.

"We was so sweaty," I say. "Man was we a shiver
that day."

She took my hand.

We held time there.

Burnin' up.

We was

c   o   o   l   .

PIG Talk

Musta been 7 late in the evening
when I come home.
Hit two steps up when Tiny Lewis
call out to me.

He a few stoops over.
Jamming up his cell.
Brother ain't never been more of a
busy-gossip than Tiny Lewis.

"What you need?" I ask.

"You got cops in your place," he say.

"Fo' real?"

He still going on his text.

"Brother, I don't play about cops," he say.
"They were at Mighty Mildred's, then climb
stairs to your place."

"How long they been sitting?" I ask.

He scratch his scruff.
Blow smoke of his skinny cigar.

"Not long," he say. "What you gonna do?"

I thought on it.
I could step out.
Hang at the hideout house.
Try to dodge 'em.
But they'd be back.
Too much tension.
Too much marching.
And that picture on CNN.
It circulating.

Man . . .

"Thanks for the notice," I say to Tiny.

He grin his fake gold grill.

"Always try to help a brother," he say.

And he right back on his phone spreading

half-truth.

I come up in the apartment.
Two cops sitting wait on the couch.

"You didn't answer my text," say Monica,
her voice stretched fake in its tone.

"My phone drizzled," I say.

Cops that come up in West Split
don't treat you way they do South Pear kids.
Pigs that come here
step right up in your space like they own it.
Always one black and one white.
Salt and Pepper, we call 'em.
Always with a badge flash and a gun glance
just so you know
they run however long you with 'em.

Only I knew these two po-lice.
That hospital po-lice and another from
when Tony lose breath.

"They wanna talk a few. About Ricky-Ricky,"
say Monica.

Monica, she nervous.
And 'cause I know her for being cool,
that make me nervous too.
I keep my eyes steady on the po-lice.

"Theodore Todd Clark," say Pepper. "Last I seen
you, everything was clean."

"Still is," I say.

Pepper one of the cops work the case
where Tony get faded.
He always squeeze at me to roll on who done it.
They had masks.
They come quick.
I just couldn't know.

And Pepper and me,
we both black, but
skin don't make you the same.
I didn't
trust him then and don't now.
Not by a long-ass mile.

"Theodore," say Salt. "We met a few days
ago at the hospital."

"Yeah . . ." I say. "I got memory."

"Good," say Salt. "Because we've had a number of
eyewitnesses unable to report what happened in front of" —
he referred to his notes — "the Wooden Spoon."

I look at Pepper.
He watching me close.

Salt had his pen and li'l notepad ready fo'

the good writing. The ink hovering over
the blank square of white.

"Can you tell us who was involved in the fight?"
ask Salt.

Now all I had to do was point the finger at
Money Mike.
They'd arrest him.
He go up in front of the judge with a lawyer
that some big money up the Jive chain pay fo'.
He'd make bail.
And then pop the guys and me and maybe even
Nia if he knew I feel for her.
Not spray bullets himself 'cause Mike could
convince some young Jive to do it.
Some kid that wouldn't have to do large time
or might skip out all together if he slick enough.

I knew this game.

I wasn't gonna play it like that.

"I went over to help Ricky-Ricky," I say.
"'Cause I seen him flat."

And I did see him.
I did see him laying there
on my floor between us.
Like he was . . .
alive-dying that moment.

"I just step to him," I say. "Shake on him.
See if he have breath."

I seen Tony.
In the store. Squeezing that bread to strangle.
Blood coming out his head.

"He was gone," I say to Salt.

Tony's light just went.
Ricky-Ricky . . . he was wet with blood.

"Then I got hit, and it all went to nuthin'," I say.

Salt and Pepper kept strong eyes on me.

"So . . ." say Pepper, "you didn't see who
beat Richard Moses?"

"Who?"

"Ricky-Ricky," say Pepper.

"Nah . . ." I say. "I just seen him flat. He a
good kid, you know? He never drop a bad
thought on nobody."

"Theodore," say Salt, "I can see you care about
Richard. I've got to be honest. I think you
aren't telling us everything. Now, c'mon."

And there he went.

Making sincere with his brow.
And guess what?

I
AIN'T
NO

FOOL!

Salt was the epitome of why I ain't trust on po-lice
Salts. Most of 'em make like we're all on the even,
but we ain't. Pepper knows that and he'd rather make
nice with Salts and keep his flash badge than be in
the muck with the hood rats.
He from West Split and will do whatever it takes
to remind you he ain't anymore.

No favors.
No black-on-black knuckle bump.
He assimilate.

"It's all I know," I say.

Monica step, "He told you what he know.
We hurtin' for Mildred. Everyone is. But
that's all Theo knows."

Salt and Pepper weren't sold.

"I wasn't look to dig," I say. "It wasn't my cool."

Scribble, scribble. Salt's pen went.
Pepper held eyes on me. He was the one to fear.

He hated me for being a West Split.
Nothing was gonna change my ZIP code for him.

"So, you were trying to help Richard Moses?" ask Salt.

"He said that already," Monica pipe out.

Pepper glare her way. "Maybe we should speak with him
alone."

"He fifteen," she say. "I let you in to keep it clear, but he
doesn't have to feed you all anything."

Monica was smart and willing to word dig
when it came down to the Pigs. They'd done
her wrong once and once all it took.
Monica like Hilda that way.
One and done.
Then you marked out forever. Ask Buffalo that.

"Look, I don't know nuthin' 'cept what I told you," I say.

Pepper leaned in. "Here's what I'm feeling. You
standing there, looking me eye to eye and laying out
some straight fiction. I don't like it when the story don't
make it."

I was in deep and knew it. Damn, Ricky-Ricky. What
you tell Money Mike to make him flat-fix you on the
real and leave me in this mess?

Pepper sprung up outta the couch like some snake in the

wild on TV. Only his fangs
were brick-thick mitts fo' hands.
He hooked under my arm.
His grab was deep.

"Hey," say Monica.

"Get outta my way, girl," say Pepper.

"Girl?"

She was on fire now.

"He's gonna sit for us down at the precinct," say Pepper.

"Get off me," I say. "I tried to help that kid."

Pepper shoved me face-fucking-first into the wall.

Snap.
          Lock.
Cuffed!

"Get off him," Monica say.

Salt say, "Tell your mom that he'll be at the downtown
precinct."

Pepper dragged me full-flail and raged.
Oh, did it hurt my side, but I so mad it didn't change
my move.

"I didn't do nuthin' wrong," I say. "I try to help him."

They dragged me down the hall.

"Call Hilda!" I shout to Monica.

"I got you, T," she say. "You keep it close. Real close."

They drag me down the stairs.
I wasn't having none of that be-a-good-boy shit.
But I kept my mouth shut when Pepper
tempt my speak.

I seen Tiny Lewis
dropping the report on his cell soon
as they drag me out the door.

"I got your story, T," say Tiny Lewis.

They pull me 'round the corner to a squad car.
Detective po-lice don't drive squads.
They open the door.
Jimmy, Catch, and Yo-Yo, they was in there.
Salt and Pepper crunched me in too.

There wasn't no room to breathe up in that ride.
I twisted to try and loosen
the pull on my side. Them cuffs were gonna
unstitch me. Complete!

"What is this?" I say to 'em.

"You spill?" ask Catch.

"Hell, nah," I say.

"You don't say shit," say Catch.

"Don't rub me," I say to Catch.

"T, keep your calm," say Jimmy.

I give Jimmy ears.

"The po-lice aren't being clean," he say. "They wanna pin this. They hold speak to me about the burnin' up on Strawberry Lane."

"I'm scared, y'all," say Yo-Yo. "I'm sick-scared."

"Shut up!" say Catch. "You shut that shit down. And all of you. They gonna divide to conquer. We don't say shit."

"Ain't nuthin' to say," I say. "We ain't hurt nobody."

I look to Yo-Yo.
Brother turnin' white on being so scared.

"It's gonna be cool, Yo-Yo," I say. "Try to breathe if you can find it."

I sure was trying to find a breath from all the pain I feelin'.

"Hey," say Catch. "Keep the story clear. Ricky-Ricky
got robbed by some 'burb kid lookin' for powder.
That's all we know."

"No," I say.

"This ain't a negotiate," say Catch.

"I'm down to speak what needs to be, but I ain't
spinning no words to make Ricky-Ricky out thug.
All we say is we come up and seen him flat. That's all."

Two po-lice get set up in the front seat.

"Good thing you're all friends," say the Driver Cop.
"It's a tight fit back there."

He roll out the engine.
Hard!

"One of you spills," whispers Catch. "And we ended.
Feel me?"

We all nodded.
We had one story.
The only story we'd need to remember.

Cops blasted the sirens.
They wanted to make us the show.

As we frenzy outta the hood, they cruised us past
the Wooden Spoon, and you know that shit was straight

up on purpose. They wanted the Jives to see the four of us
jammed up in that Pig mobile.
They wanted everyone in the hood to know
who squealed.
Money Mike's eyes held hard to mine.

Just like that.
I was just as good as enlisted.
We was definitely in it

n   o   w   .

Pigville

They run Jimmy, Yo-Yo, Catch, and me in
these separate rooms at Pigville. Just like Catch
said they would. I'd been there before.
Once 'cause some lady said she was robbed by a
black kid with a black hoodie runnin' to West Split.
Guess I matched the description being black and
wearing a hoodie.
They lined me up with a bunch of guys I didn't
know.
She said I wasn't black enough, and they let me go.
That was rich.

Today.
I didn't know the Pigs' game on the real.
All I knew fo' sure was that Ricky-Ricky died.

How he died wasn't on me to spit.
Ever!
'Less I wanted it all to end six feet deep from
the Jives. Cross 'em and you wish someone else
hung you.

The reflection of my bust-up face in the "mirror"
caught me off. Hilda was straight on. I did look
part Frankenstein. Bruised and puffed up.
Like my dad when we seen him in the morgue.
He'd been blue too long to do anything for him.
Trust.
I tried.
Even though I seen him die.
When I put eyes on him stretched flat and cold,
it just shake out my know.
I grab on him. Make like I could
warm him back to breath.

Hilda jus' let me go on fo' 'while.
She see how it do me to lose Tony.
Truth?
When we leave the morgue, I still hadn't get
how it do her.
She ain't been full since.
Maybe I ain't been neither.

There was chat-chat under the door.
Shadows peeled.
They always wanna scare you in Pigville. Keep
you waiting with nothing to drink—eat. Drop
your sugar to taint your think.

They got angles.
They ain't being legit.

The hum-flicker of the shit lights and smell of
dried piss and old coffee make me itch and squirm,
but I hold steady 'cause
that mirror I see myself in wasn't no mirror.
It go reverse, and I knew those Pigs had some D.A.-
type lawyer-pimp on the other side.
They caged me up in that room.
Watching the animal like it was zoo time. I
wasn't gonna give 'em a show.
Nah.
I'm not the beast they make me out to be.
They'll see.

Pepper and Salt rolled up, sliding and grinding
the chairs.
Salt slapped my file on the table.
Yeah, I had a file.
Nuthin' like Catch's.
You could bind his book-style
'cause it was so thick.
Not that anyone would wanna read
about the kind of stuff he'd done.
Or really, what been done to him.

"Theodore Todd Clark. Quite a file here," say Salt.
He picked through the pages. "You've been involved
with the Jives before."

I held my head high, shoulders back.
This was the part where they try to shame you
for being a "bad kid," only I hadn't done nuthin' to be bad kid fo'.
Not this time. 'Cept try and help a good kid
who done fooled himself to think he could make sweet
or large or somethin' with 'em guys.
Damn Ricky-Ricky.
Fuck.

"Want to tell me about that love mark there on
your hand?" ask Salt.

Salt was fixated on the ink I cover
every chance I find.

"It ain't how you think," I say.

"That's a Jive tattoo, isn't it?" ask Salt.

Talk about fool—I felt it.
Day Money Mike mark me, he was up
on some kinda high.
Say the ink was to protect, but he lied.
It was to make me a slave.

"I'm not rollin' on anybody," I say. "'Cause I got
nuthin' to roll. And that ink ain't me."

But it almost been me.

Money Mike didn't have to work too hard

to stick that Jive brand in my skin.
Tony done been dropped.
We was hurtin' for things like rent money and food
and even though I was sure a Jive cut Tony down,
Mike kept saying, "You off, T. Jive don't drip out a
guy like Tony."

And I wanted to believe him.
I thought if I had that ink maybe I could.
Maybe I'd stop being on the think that he had some
part in all it.
I mean, shit. He my brother.

"Here's how this is gonna work," say Pepper.
"You gonna give me three, and you go free."

Three for free? That's some shit.
You give up three people, and you will
never
be free again.
Nobody spills from West Split.
Be better to do ten solid in the Pen 'fore
squealing on guys like Money Mike or Jay Ridge.
'Cause streets hold court.
You guilty from the step and no point of calling innocent.
Pepper know that.

He ain't no fool.

"It's your choice," say Salt. "Your friends are
ready to talk."

"Then why you in here?" I ask. "If they spitting,
you don't need to deal me."

"I think you're a smart kid, Theodore," say Salt. "We
want to help you."

"You wanna help me?" I ask. "How come when shit
goes down, black-and-white don't show fo' a hour?
When my neighbor's sister got raped, you all blamed it
on how she dress. 'Cause the guy that force her
was some Nabisco cracker from the 'burb."

Pepper slammed his hand against the table.
He got some heat.

"Your injustice doesn't matter to me, *boy*.
Now you can roll and walk or we'll give another try
with one of your friends," say Pepper.

This ain't no cop TV show.
Po-lice don't have to keep it real and clear
'less the camera on 'em.
Ain't no camera up in here.
'Less it were back behind that glass.
My feeling was there wasn't no camera.
Not how Pepper be all in a roar.
And that guy was hungry.
Only I don't feed Pigs.

"It isn't like you haven't done it before," say Salt.

Then I got it.
They were lookin' fo' a big pinch.
Not any three. They wanted the big three.
Money Mike plus Jay Ridge plus—nah.
I'm sittin' on this.

"You thought a Jive had something to do
with your father's murder," say Pepper. "I got it
straight here from the interview."

"I never said that."

"But you suspected," Salt say. "Says right here. Witness,
Theodore Todd Clark, believes that a member of the Jives,
in which his brother, Michael Clark, is affiliated, shot
their father, Anthony Michael Clark."

"That ain't on," I say. "My words have twist."

"Stop speaking in that street foolness," say Pepper. "This
is how you dropped it down the night you were
interviewed by me."

They was setting up something.
I could feel it in their motivation.

"It also states," says Salt, "that your father had an
altercation two days prior to the shooting with
Carnegie Joseph Moses. Can you tell us about that?"

"What's that got to do with Ricky-Ricky?" I ask.

"Did you witness the fight with"—Salt be reading—
"Big Joe?"

"There wasn't no fight or altercation," I say. "Tony
was even with everybody. He never dig. It ain't
his cool."

Salt chuckled.
I wasn't making on his funny.

"Here's the thing, Theodore," say Salt. "Big Joe
is Ricky-Ricky's brother. The kid you're telling us
you tried to help."

"That's how it go," I say.

"So, you wouldn't have attacked Ricky-Ricky to
get back at one of the leaders of the gang you've
stated you believe killed your father?"

"My words got twist," I say. "That ain't how I suggest
it."

I wasn't down with none of it.
They working that angle clear.
Trying to pin Ricky-Ricky getting flat-fixed on me?
Word.
That's just not gonna happen.

"Tony did hold speak with Big Joe," I say. "It
didn't go down in some altercation. They had
knowing of each other from time gone long."

"And . . . ?" ask Pepper.

"That's it," I say.

They wasn't believin' and wasn't mine to educate
'em.
Tony ask Big Joe,
black-to-black,
if he'd cool the recruit of Money Mike.

Big Joe, how it was told to me, kept close respect
for Tony. Say outside drugs, Tony the only one
running hope in the hood.

But when Mike get sound that Tony ask Big Joe
to drop him loose, he mad.
Say it make him look weak.
And man did they go at it.
Hilda demand on Tony to take the belt to Money.
Hell. Let's be real.
She wanna take it on him too.

Monica trying to keep the peace.
But there was no doin'.
Mike always wanted what he didn't have.
And when he got offer to enlist with the Jives . . .
ride up in a big car . . . pocket big green.

He wasn't just a hood brother wishin' fo' more.
Shit.
He *was* the more.

'Cause Mike eager on money and smart on slingin'.
And he knew how to play the cops and the law.
He wasn't full grown into his anger back then.
But he know how to bend something to his will.
Guys flooding the drugs in the hood dig on that.
They like the way Mike sweat venom.

So there Mike go . . . movin' up big.
Got him a sweet ride.
Got him a girl or two or three.
His whole life on this rotation of watches
and phones and
sneaks
and all he had to do was keep people hooked on the
needle or the powder or the pipe.

And Tony . . .
he wasn't down on none of it.
Both his brothers enlisted when they was kids.
One got popped, and the other sent up fo' big time . . .
Life!

So Tony tell Mike as much on that kinda style of being.
But Mike didn't give a fuck 'cause he done tasted
the ladies and liquor and he like it.
He like it a lot!

There come a knock on the door, and Salt
slid out of the chair.
He hold time between the door and hall.
Talking to some woman in a suit.

Her making attention to me.
And Pepper?
That brother was thick on breaking me.
He a rottweiler that wanted to dogfight the shit outta me.

I didn't cower.

Salt make step and whispered to Pepper.

It wasn't long 'fore Monica and Hilda come bustin'
through the door with some stable, freebie lawyer.

"I know you didn't drag my son out of his *home* on
no charges," say Hilda.

"Ma'am, we are investigating a murder case," say Salt.
"I spoke with you at the hospital—"

"I got memory, Detective Kelly. I'm not misinformed."

The lawyer made lawyer speak that meant I was
free to go.

"You arresting my son?" ask Hilda.

"You okay, T?" ask Monica.
I nodded.

Salt try to play nice on Hilda by saying, "We suspect
Theodore was involved or knows who was involved with—"

"Let me stop you there," say Hilda. "Did you read him
his rights?"

The cops had been had by Hilda A. Clark.

"I know who you are," she say to Pepper. "You pull
my son out of his home with no cause again,
and I will raise hell on this earth."

We walked on out quick.
Like we was all running from our death.

"What did you say to them?" Monica ask.

"I kept it quiet," I say. "Hilda, I didn't do
no wrong. Fo' real."

Hilda wasn't giving me no voice.
She still burned up at me fo' turnin' quick
at her.

"I sure hope you are on the real," say Monica.

"You know I is," I say.

We get outside, where Smokey waiting with a
cool-brother lean against his car.

"What up, Smokey?" I ask, throwing him a nod.

"How is you, Young Black?"

"Man, 'em cops be raging," I say.

"Get in the car," say Hilda. "We ain't got no time
to be standing."

We drive away from the precinct.
Past big tinted-window buildings,
and guys strutting the sidewalk in suits . . . ties.
We roll past some homeless brothers hangin'
outside the main public library,
catching a smoke.
We drive up on the interstate and past South Pear.
'Fore too long, we leave the good and cross back on over
into the hood.

"Here's how this is all going down," say Hilda.
"Say your good-byes. I'm taking you by train
to Houston."

"No," I say.

"Hold your thoughts right now," she say. "It's how it
is, and you better get warm to it. We leaving after the
Fourth."

"That the deal you making with Mike?" I ask.
"I know you holding speak behind me."

She look over her shoulder at me fierce.

"That's the deal I made with God and your father.

Now leave it loose before I send you to both of
them tonight," she say.

I settle back
and
spin rage up inside.

Damn, Ricky-Ricky!
      Damn!
            Damn!

      Damn, you fool!

Hilda Run the Show

Houston.
That's where Hilda started
and finished her sentence.

It don't matter if it after midnight.
She been going loud since 'fore Smokey
drop us
u
  p
    the
        s
      r
     i
    a
   t
s

and not letting me pursue a word one-time.

She flung her purse up on the kitchen table.
Step outta her shoes.
She ain't slow down to catch a breath.
Go straight to the box fan and get it going.
We all a sweaty mess.

"This heat gonna end us," she say, marching
direct to the fridge.

She pour out a large cup of sweet tea.
Drinking it deep.
Her thirst had no stop,
just go.
I was still raging, though.
Still mad as Juice Box's dog upstairs.

"Hilda—" I say.

Only her hand go up while she finish her drink.

"You going to Texas and that's the truth, Theo," she say.
"Your cousins live one hour out. No gangs. No guns.
Just cows and Dairy Queens."

"Hilda, please," I say. "Just give me relief."

"Relief?" she say. "You come up here like your brother—"

"What?" I ask.

"Don't you 'what' at me," she warn. "You put hands on me in my home."

"Hilda," say Monica.

"Don't you make excuse for him," Hilda say to her.

Hitting on Hilda
ain't nuthin' I mean. I
just react.
I ain't my brother.
I ain't nuthin' like him.

We all held our quiet a moment.

"Hilda, I been needing to hold speak with you
on that," I say. "But you don't wanna give me no time."

But she was definitely on to give me hard eyes.

"I owe you apologies," I say. "Fo' how I swing at you."

She toss the cup in the sink.

"You owe me apologies for a lot."

"How's that?" I ask. "See, you can't hear nuthin'
I speak. You—"

Monica step between.

"We all need to simmer," she say.

"I ain't even started to boil," say Hilda.

"Just give him some air," Monica say.

"So, I should let him walk like you did. Get
his stitch ripped by Michael."

"Why you need to spar?" ask Monica. "He
fifteen. Nearly sixteen. He trying to make
sense of this place."

Hilda march up on Monica.
I thought she might strike her down.
Her hand was definitely hot and
looking to cool it on someone's face.

"Hilda, I know you don't get me, don't respect me
and wish I did you right a hundred and fifty-one
different ways," Monica say. "But you need to settle
that rage you got with him and me and Tony, who can't
be here. The streets are on fire. We can't change that
right now. If you on for him to go to Houston, wait a few
weeks. Let me labor and give this baby a life. I'll make
step with him."

Hilda shook her head and paced it out.

"We can't wait on you," say Hilda. "It's all too close.
He marked."

"I'm over everybody makin' deals where I be going,"
I say. "I can't run. I can't be no skipper."

And that definitely sent Hilda to boil.

"I tell you some truth," say Hilda. "I'm frayed.
My edges are loose, but I'm on what's right.
Don't you put eyes to the floor. You give me
attention."

She all up on me.
I wasn't feeling none of that.
Fo' real.

"I hear why you try and help Ricky-Ricky. And truth?
I can't fault that. It is what your daddy would do.
But hear me straight. I got one purpose in this life
till you grown, and that's to be sure you get grown.
Your brother hateful and rageful and he not right
in his heart. He playin' you so far 'cause he havin'
fun or some senseless thing, but that ain't gonna
hold time forever."

She sit it out at the table.
The way her body held made Hilda to be smaller
than I ever take to notice.

"I'm tired," say Hilda. "Tired of the po-lice taking our
black men and women. Putting them in deep, dark time."

She turn to me.
Her eyes full of water.

"They building a cell right now 'cause the color
your skin. I cannot let you be the fool, Theodore."

Hilda defeated.
Straight up and down the middle defeated.
Her shoulders cut forward.
Her breath shake.

She put eyes to the time.
It was all her good effort to stand up.

"Y'all need to go to bed," she say.

Monica made step to her room.
Hilda shut off the light and wasn't far behind.
And me?

I stood there in the dark.
Listening to the clink of the window fan.
Sirens and speak from the street.
Juice Box's dog barking and scratching.
Everything all mashed up together,
separate.

Then
I hear a pop,
  an echo . . . some bang-noise in the distance
and wondered if someone just got
d
  r
    o
      p
        p
          e
            d.

Would I be

n e x t ?

What Do They Know?

Jimmy text me early.
Sleep still concrete in the edges of my eyes.
He say Hilda make call to all their folks soon
as she got news we been picked up.
Jimmy made go outta the precinct not too long after me.
But Yo-Yo and Catch's mom left them down there
extra hours, so they just been cut loose.

I kept low at the abandon house.
Waiting for all 'em to show.
Dropping a li'l word to Nia.
Letting her know what went down with the
po-lice 'cause she drop word asking.
Even though I explain how I was straight

on all of it, it feel like she not accepting my truth.
Which really spin me off.

"What up?" say Jimmy, coming up
the basement stairs.

"Man," I say, "it's real to see you." I
tuck him in for a hug.

"I know, right?"

Yo-Yo and Catch come up behind.

"I thought we all pinched," say Jimmy.

"What up, T," say Yo-Yo.

Me and Yo-Yo shook it out
while Catch looked harder than ever.

"What up, Catch?" I say.

"It's all even," he say.

Nuthin' was even 'bout him.
He be raised up in his think.
Could see it in how he hold stance.

"What you guys speak?" I ask.

"We all stick to what we say," say Jimmy.
"Nobody rolled on nothing."

"That don't mean they won't be on," say
Yo-Yo.

"Stop with your punk-fool, fear-ass shit," Catch
say to Yo-Yo. "You on the worry twenty-four/seven, and it's
rubbing me."

Yo-Yo . . . he actually shove Catch.
I mean, brother fo' real threw all he got into it.

Catch, he intimidating.

"Fat-ass," say Catch.

He bring Yo-Yo forward with a grin.

Yo-Yo was burnin', and he shove him again.
He shove the grin almost outta Catch.

"Guys . . ." say Jimmy.

"You mad, fat-ass?" say Catch.

And Yo-Yo make to swing,
but it didn't land nuthin' 'cept air.

Catch punch him direct in the gut.

"Stop!" I say.

Catch couldn't be crushed.
He punched him again.

That's when I hit Catch across the back.
His back was hurtin' mean.
His angle was disrupt.

"Y'all baby him," he say to us. "You don't make him no favors."

"Your style ain't clean on this," I say. "So he ain't broke down hard like you? He still got fear. At least he real."

Catch step to me.

"Seriously, cool it," say Jimmy to Catch.

"Step to me," I say. "'Cause I ain't timeless."

"No more diggin'," say Jimmy. "Damn, we friends. We ain't animals. We ain't soldiers. What's on with you?"

Catch held his cool with Jimmy between.
Yo-Yo scrambled up to his feet and cut out.

"It ain't no good fo' you 'less you crush everyone's think that don't set up with yours," I say.

"The po-lice," say Catch. "They want your brother. They want Jay Ridge. They want some Jives all the way up to Big Joe."

"What did you do?" I ask.

"It's their speak, bro," Catch say. "I just nod."

If we weren't all marked before, Catch had secured
our graves. He done opened his think on the hood
to the po-lice.

"We in the war," say Catch. "Fuck Iraq. Fuck all
that foreign shit. It's these streets."

"Look," say Jimmy. "We all come here to be in the know.
But we can't be on like we enlisted. We need to be cool.
Ride all this till it hit empty."

Catch get up on Jimmy.
He never do Jimmy up in his face.
Never!

"You live softer than any us, Hoop Dreams,"
say Catch. "My truth don't have my mama—"

"You crossing it," warn Jimmy.

But Catch couldn't be cooled.
Jimmy try to shake the space loose between the
two of 'em, but Catch continue his step.

He be intent!

"Your *mama*, who straddle the hood but cater

to the good so her son can bus it to play ball.
So, don't tell me to ride all this out. The
muthafucking storm ain't dissipating.
We is the storm."

Catch stepped it back.

"Y'all living the lie," he say. "Y'all need to get smart
to it."

He jet on upstairs.
Got to chewing minutes on his cell immediate.

"We marked," I say to Jimmy.

Jimmy put some space between us.
Pacing out his think. Scratching
at the knuckles of his cast.

"I dunno what to think on nothing, man," he say.
I'm tired of all this noise. Catch be losing his sane.
You and him. You's best friends."

Jimmy be distraught over his think.

"He so mad at you, T."

"Fo' what?" I ask.

"Not being him. I dunno."

"Forget that," I say. "I ain't cutting nobody down.

I ain't no soldier. This ain't my war."

"I hear that," say Jimmy.

His phone start to popping.
He was rolling messages and throwing
'em back.

"Ask you something?" I say.

He give me attention.

"Hilda want me to jet. Go to Houston. Would you?"

He shrug.

"They got basketball and ladies in Houston?" he ask.

I laugh a li'l.

"Yeah," I say.

And there Jimmy go.
Grinning that cool-brother grin.

"Shit," he say. "We seen hard before. This will all
snooze. Just gotta keep our cool. Stop tearing
each other down."

He put his hand on my shoulder.
Holding his attention for confirmation.

"Yeah . . ." I say. "You on."

"Let's see if we can find Yo-Yo," he say.
"Guy owes me a milk shake."

And Jimmy and me,
we headed out.

Leaving Catch
a   l   o   n   e   .

The Wooden Spoon

It was sometime after 2 a.m. when
I hear the sirens go off.
I stumble, stupid-sleepy, to my window.

Fire trucks and po-lice speeding down
the street.

People was coming out of their sleep just
like me. Trying to see what was on.
When they all start to follow the scene,
I threw on my jeans and kicks and
unlock the gate on the window and stepped.

The fire-glow pulsed three blocks away.

Smoke, twist-curl reaching into the street
light, star-strangled sky.

It was something.

Closer I stepped, the more I knew.
Everyone was buzzing like gnats.
Someone had set the Wooden Spoon to flame.

Half the hood stood street corner to street corner.
All watching that one-time good memory,
turn Jive territory go up in

f l a m e s .

Flames that lit up the whole damn block.
Fire fingers stretched up to the sky.
Smoke crumbling out.
Sparks of rough orange-yellow glow
popping—dancing loose and limber
across the night air.
Walls collapsed into one another.

Had Money Mike been inside?
Did a deal go wrong? Was it payback?

> "Just let the damn thing burn!"
> shouted a woman. "Let it burn straight
> to hell and back."

I seen Smokey pull up in his car.

The fire-glow breathe all over him. I
seen Old Man Charlie in his robe.
I seen people from the meeting at the
church.

I seen people I didn't even know.
Who was all these faces I didn't know
watching the Wooden Spoon burn?

Brothers with bandannas on their faces
and reflect shades over their eyes.
Arms outstretched V for victory.
Cheering, only we wasn't at a football game
or whatever.

We was watching our own hood burn.
Exploding glass.
Firemen hosing it with all they got.

And right where Ricky-Ricky drop,
just behind one of them fire trucks, is
where I seen it.
S P R A Y E D out on the ground.

RICKY-RICKY R.I.P.

Out of the corner my eye, I seen Catch.
His face ignited up good by the burnin' light.
And he had this . . . way in his stance.
His smile—his eyes.

That's how I knew.

He'd been the one fool enough to torch
the Wooden Spoon.

With the strike of a match,
he'd started a

w   a   r   .

Time to Wake Up

It was early.
Real early when Catch unhook the latch
on the window gate.
I sprung up,
snapping the baseball bat Tony
give me when I was seven.

Catch just laugh.
He fake like he scared of my swing.

"What—are you off?" I ask.

"Nah, man . . ." he say.

He floating fo' sure. His walk had angles.

"You high?" I ask.

"Shit, nah. You know I don't abuse."

I lean to him.
Me, holding my side good.

"Seriously?" I say.

He been drinking big time.
He smell like a bottle of 40 and whiskey.

"Kicked back over at Nacho's after the
campfire," he say.

I crawl back in bed.

"We ain't at camp, Catch. Everything gonna get
turned up."

I couldn't get comfortable.
Every move I make something else go to hurt on me.

"We need to speak, T."

"It's early, Catch. I need to knock off."

"It's late, man."

He wasn't gonna let me sleep,
so I prop against the wall.
He drew up a seat on a chair.

"What you need to speak?" I ask. "'Cause
my tired is long, and I ain't in no mood to
push and pull with you."

"You know, yesterday. When I got heated with
you."

I stretch out my neck.
Try to limber up.
Everything so tight.

"Sorry I step hard," he say. "Fighting with you,
it ain't my cool. Shit, man."

Catch
put eyes out the window.
Watching the nuthin' down below.

"Everything so upside and straight to hell down,"
he say. "I had this feelin' DJ Spin gonna get dropped,
but I couldn't speak it to him. Even knowing if
he get dropped, then my chance to spit music was over.
That some deal, right?"

I nodded.

"I know your situation at home is tense," I say.
But you gotta quit fighting, man. Fighting everybody.
The way you squash with Yo-Yo. He ain't done
you wrong *ever*."

Catch lean to one side.

He lose his center trying to hold his think.

"I can't always protect him," say Catch.

"So you tear a brother down?" I ask.

"I dunno," he say. "Shit, man."

He make steps and sit it out on the bed.

"Yo-Yo, he tell you he wants to get up outta here?"
Catch ask.

I nodded.

"Maybe he's on," say Catch. "Maybe we could
get some kind of restart. Do-over kinda thing."

What was I gonna say?
Even drunk to the sky, he was still
Catch. The guy always prop me up when
I wanna drop. But still.
I dunno.

"You guys wanna run and Hilda wants me to
skip to Houston. Why can't we all just be even,
you know? Like . . . why we gotta be scared to
hold still?"

Catch chuckle.

"'Cause that's some storybook bullshit, man."

"Why can't it be different? The way Tony talk?"

"Tony dead, man," say Catch. "He ain't talkin'."

And that cut me on the deep.
To hear it spoke out.
I knew Tony gone.
I knew he ain't up in the ceiling of all 'em
places Hilda hold speak with him.
Still.
He'd know how to set this all straight.

"Man, I don't wanna fight with you," say Catch.
"Cool?"

"Yeah," I say. "Cool."

As tired as I be, I easy, knowing we made
some kind of agreement not to be brutal.
That shit wear me completely out.

"Can I lay it out for a bit?" ask Catch.
"I don't wanna deal with Pinky. Too spent to
walk to the crackhouse."

"C'mon," I say. "I'll grab the couch fo' few.
We leaving fo' the funeral at nine thirty.
Want me to shake you?"

"Nah, I'll be out the window by then."

I hung at the door a sec.

Couldn't let my mind not ask.

"Catch?"

"What?"

"Why you burn it?"

"Maybe I didn't," he say.

He ease cozy up on my blanket.
Sliding that Smoker under the pillow.

"But if I did, ain't gonna ever hold speak on it.
Especially to Money Mike's li'l brother, who
everyone know would be ended for knowing."

Catch curl up in my bed.
You wouldn't of known he wasn't a kid
when he drop off.
Nothing hard and broken and hurtin' and angry.
He just another kid.

S l e e p i n'.

Mildred Breaks My Heart

(choir singing, mournful-like)
They callin' his name / They callin' his name
Young man claimed
Too early / Too soon . . .
To Heaven's Gates
Oooh
Heaven's Gates
Where his heart can reign . . .

The choir been praising notes since
'fore we come in the church door.
Nine women and four men.
Go from one song to the next. They
was on with so much sorrow in
their voices
almost everyone spilt tears.

Monica, Hilda, and me.
We hold seats a few rows from the front.
Place packed up tight.
Shoulder to West Split shoulder.
People was hurtin'.

And there he was.
Richard Moses. Ricky-Ricky to all us.
Stretched out quiet
and cold
with the casket closed.
A printed-up photo of him propped up high.
Him grinning so big.

Mighty Mildred, who marched on Washington
and gather people to so much change,
she so small, sitting in that front pew.

Sitting alone.

Watching her make my heart break.
Down the middle and to the sides
cracked.

She always on me to keep on in school. She
say, "Listen to the Lord, listen to your mama,
and listen to your father. Don't get hard on
wanting a girl too quick. Don't get loose
on waiting on a girl too long."

Mildred wasn't relative by any blood,
but she always take me in like we was.

Maybe that's what sparked it in me
to stand.
Stand with Hilda and Monica
making eyes to follow what I was doing.

> *He's not ashamed / Of the life he make*
> *He's not to blame / For the way he was*
> *'Cause to his Lord / He nothing but love . . .*

I took time right beside Mildred.
She didn't share eyes with me.
She hold so quiet.
Her back bent forward doing all it
could to keep her from falling to the floor.

I took her closed-up hand
the way she did mine when Tony get buried.

I wanted to say somethin' to give her ease.
All I could do was hold space and her hand.
That's all I know.

Then she held my hand good and intent.
She straighten up her back and sat tall.

Man, she was fierce.
I respect her so much, I can't even say.

Choir pick up the beat and everyone take
stance.

> *The day has come / The day has come*

The day has come / To bring him home
Bring him home / Ooooh, bring him home
Richard Moses . . . / We walk with you
Richard Moses . . . / We walk with you
Go on home . . . / Go on home
Go on home
Go, go, go . . . / Go on home . . .

Reverend took time to share his grief
and heartache.
Reading a li'l Scripture and
making a lotta thought on how Ricky-Ricky
was happy where he gone.

He invite Mighty Mildred to take to the
microphone.
She patted my hand and make her way up.

She stood there all frail and small but
big inside and say, "I appreciate all you comin'
to see Richard off on Fourth of July. I expect you
had other plans of where to be."

Mighty Mildred held her quiet.
Her hands grip the podium intense.

"This year, I was gonna drive out to the Lakes," she
say. "As many of you know, that takes some time.
Richard always wanted to see the Lakes. He'd be on
about them. Wanting to splash in the water.
He loved the idea of it."

We all held our quiet between tears.
Shit.
Even I cry.

"And you all know my feelin' of love for you,"
say Mighty Mildred. "Meals you bring me and people
come to sit with me. My heart ain't strong enough
to make this loss alone. No, Lord, it is not."

She gather her think.
We all held in grief.

"But last night, as I make my first true effort to rest since
losing Richard, our community was charred to wake," she say.
"Someone from our community or maybe another burn
the Wooden Spoon down. They spray-painted
RICKY-RICKY R.I.P. But that message doesn't give me
a moment of ease. Burning any part of this community
does not help Richard rest in peace. He a kind soul.
We all know he was touched off in his thoughts.
But he never would want you to hurt someone or some
place in his name. You all feel me?"

                              "We love you, sister Mildred!"
                              shout a woman from the back.

"Kindness and peace, sister Kim," she answer back.
"Now, I know we all want justice. I'd be lying to say
my ears don't hear the speak around West Split.
But violence. That is not my hope. Go to the streets.
Tell our story, but not with fire and guns and hate. We
cannot have . . . no more . . . dead black babies."

And that's when she just let go.
She just couldn't hold good no more.
The Reverend step to her quick.
Hold her steady.
She just fall to pieces.

Men from the congregation.
They step real fast.
Women — so many people go to help her
to her seat.
Everyone just all 'round her.

Choir went back to calling music.

That casket closed up tight.
'Cause he beat so bad.
'Cause he ain't smilin' in there.
Man, he had a way to glow.

And I try to act like I was a'ight
but I wasn't.
Couldn't be.
All this . . . all us together under the church
singing hymn and tearing up.

None of it was right.
I couldn't speak for the guys, but me . . . I
was busted up, broken inside.
Felt like I couldn't say nuthin' to nobody.
My heart just hurt.

B   r   e   a   k   .

* * *

After the service, I seen Smokey outside.
Standing near his ride.

"What up, Smokey?" I say.

"Afternoon, Young Black," say Smokey.

"Why you always with that, man? Callin' me
Young Black."

He extend grin.
One of 'em smart-brother grins.
Like he got the know down.

"Because that's what you still is. You trying to decide
what kinda man to be. Until then, you Young Black."

"Man, your think is too robust for me."

Smokey laugh.
His whole body shook when he did.

"I like you, brother," he say. "You on your way."

We stand awhile.
Watching people step from the church.
Hold speak.
Hold each other.

"Where's your mama?" ask Smokey.

"She still inside," I say. "Holding time with Mildred."

"She a good woman," Smokey say. "Your mama."

"Yeah, I guess."

He eye me tight.

"What you guess on?" he ask.

"She half-hear me, man. That other half makes . . .
makes it tense between us."

Smokey consider.
Cross his arms and stretch his shoulders.
He had size.

"It ain't easy being a black woman in her situation,"
Smokey say. "Man, it ain't easy being a woman."

I laugh.

"Hey, a brother can imagine," he say. "Here's the thing.
She love you to every possible end of this earth."

Fo' real, she could love me less as far as I was level.
Whatever to get her to hear me more and get hot less.

"Yeah, I guess."

I stare at the hearse.
Hearse taking Ricky-Ricky to the ground.

"I tell you something?" I ask.

"Always, Young Black."

"Ricky-Ricky throw down one time. I was ten.
I remember 'cause I just had a birthday.
Pinky ain't met Catch's mom, so it was just
us three guys plus Ricky-Ricky. Tony said it
good to give a guy like him something to look up
to even if he older than us by three years.
So we all cruise corners back then."

I could see it.
Like I was right there.

"One day, we come outta school, right?
Jukebox Williams was the cool brother of West Split
back then. He was who kept slingers slingin'.
It was 'fore he got sent up fo' big time."

And I see the whole moment come into clear
view in my think. I could smell the pizza
from Little Rosa's. I could see all us . . .

"On this one day, Jukebox go to poking at me," I
say. "Talking about Tony being a Boy Scout.
Talking how we was *slaves* to the white-man
education. Talking, talking, talking till he got tired
of me not listening.

And then outta no defined reason he hit me
upside the head. And it ain't like Tony didn't teach

me how to dig. But Tony always say leave Jukebox
playing his own tunes. Don't look to get heated
'cause he always pack a Smoker."

"Your daddy wise," say Smokey.

"The wisest," I say. "So I kept walking.
And he hit me again.

And again.

And last time he struck me I

d
 r
  o
   p
    .

And Ricky-Ricky? He turn red fo' a dark-skinned
brother. There was no interruption in his thought.
He travel straight from cool to rage, and grab up
this piece of broken wood and *beat* on Jukebox.
He whip that wood right hard till it break.
And when it done broke, he swung his fists
and feet. Fo' a soft brother, you wouldn't know
Ricky-Ricky didn't have potential.

He was lit on rage.

Jukebox was like 'what?' He pull his Smoker, and

we all drop back. Everyone but Ricky-Ricky.

He just scream and holla. His shit was mad-crazy.
He run into the street just howling. Cars stop down.
People stand out to see what was all the noise.

Mighty Mildred come a runnin'. No joke.

Jukebox, he ain't know what hit him, so
staggered 'round, drunk-stepped. Guys from the
hood get up 'round him to get everything settled.

Not too long after, Jukebox got picked up fo'
ending somebody over a girl. And shit, he was a big
talker people said, and he open up his speak big fo'
the po-lice 'bout all kinds of hood secrets, so he had
more worries than some slow-thinking kid who whup
him with a board. And that was it.

Only time I see Ricky-Ricky fight on anybody,
and it was to keep me in one fixed piece. And you know,
I can't remember the last I gave him time. Like real time."

Smokey put his hand on my shoulder.

"Hey," he say.

It was eating me to the deep.
That kid ain't ever been nuthin' but cool to me.
Hold time when he see my mood was off.
He was a good kid.

"I let him die, Smokey," I say. "I let him leak out on the street. I
let his face puff up and get wet with blood so
I couldn't even make him out as a boy no more."

My eyes filled up.
They was ready to burst.

"It ain't how it's supposed to be," I say.

"I know," say Smokey.

And he hug me in.

"You gonna be all right, Young Black," say Smokey.
"You just gotta stay real."

Real?
Real was that funeral we all hold sit in.
That was real and hard, I just didn't
know how to hold time to it without
wetting my face with tears.
And . . .
Real was what most 'em people holdin'
sit and grief didn't get in full.
That kid, flat in the casket, he was fierce.
Not 'cause he throw down with Jukebox.
He was fierce because he lived . . .
like all them seconds of the day.

But now, him dead and all us gathered, I
just couldn't know how any of this was

gonna be—none of it made
understanding in me.

I
just couldn't
quit on the hurt of—I couldn't
shake none of it

o   u   t .

Is It Time to Jet?

I step on the Court still in my church clothes.
Sweatin' to the soaked.
Jimmy and Yo-Yo shooting hoop, sipping sodas
like nuthin' ever gone down.

"Thought you weren't coming," say Jimmy.

"I needed time. Besides, Nia gonna meet up with
me."

Jimmy drop to the three-point line and sink the
ball deep.

"You see Catch?" Jimmy ask.

"He come by my place early," I say. "My eyes
still crusty."

"Damn . . . that's rough," say Jimmy.

"I ain't seen him since supper last night," say
Yo-Yo. "He was amped."

"Yeah . . . I feel that," I say. "What y'all think
the po-lice gonna do?"

Held out my hands fo' the ball.
Jimmy check it, and I dribble out forward.
He make his defense deep.

"Hard to say, man," say Jimmy.

He try to steal the ball.
I back it up, but Jimmy jump at me direct.

"I think they up in this harder than usual 'cause
of the news be reporting on the twenty-four.
Two more shootings last night. Fire in South Pear too."

I held my dribble.
Giving both of 'em my attention.
"We know who get dropped?" I ask.
"Tiny Lewis spreading the word that it was
two Skins," Jimmy say.

Jimmy seen my face strike panic to the quick.
"Trejo wasn't one of them, T," say Jimmy.

I check the ball to Jimmy.
He working my weak defense hard.

"But all the noise and now the burnings," Jimmy
continue. "Po-lice gotta make time."

He twist around me.
Grace and Coolness
and
sink the ball fo' a jumper two.

"Wa-POW!" say Yo-Yo.

"Yeah, my side still illin'," I say.

Jimmy grin. "People in the Split want it different."

"Then why don't they offer speak?" I say, catching
my voice too loud. "We ain't even full-grown,
and we shoulder all this. It ain't how it should
be wrote."

"I'm scared, y'all," say Yo-Yo. "It ain't safe to
be nowhere. Pinky on the edge. When I'm on the
streets, I'm always looking over my shoulder thinking
the Jives are three steps too close."

Jimmy put his hand on Yo-Yo's shoulder.

"We'll figure it out," say Jimmy. "Be cool.
Besides, the Jives got enough to handle with the cops
beating down. Squad cars been cruising *a lot.*"

Yo-Yo . . . he was trembling.
I mean straight up got his hands shaking
like he comin' off the needle.

I hold up my hands fo' the ball. I
charge the basket, leap, and
d a m n !
My side.

"Man, you need to watch your game," say Jimmy.
"It got limits."

I kick the ball at him.
Leaning big on the wall.

"Hilda intent," I say.

Jimmy dribble to the free-throw line.

"What she say specific?" ask Jimmy.

"She spitting fire and ash," I say. "She saying we
outta here come the weekend."

"Houston, Texas, man," say Jimmy. "That's far."

"I ain't going. No way."

Jimmy's phone ring, and he step off the Court.

"I think you should. Go," say Yo-Yo.

"I know you want out. I know you scared, but
it don't matter where you go. Edge be everywhere."

Yo-Yo's eyes make attention all 'round. He truly was
feelin' the fear bigger than any us.

"Not like here," say Yo-Yo. "Not everywhere."

I toss him the ball. Wave him forward to make a
run for the hoop.

"You ain't got game right now, T," Yo-Yo say.

I wave him on.

He turn his ball cap bill backward.
Lower some of his mass with the dribble.
Man, he had some quick to his move when
he first got to West Split.

That's 'fore he start eating his way outta
everything that nervous his system.

"Maybe I could come see you down there," he say.

He fake-dribble right.
We was sweating mad-crazy.

"They always someone want to keep you in line,
Yo-Yo. 'Cause you black. 'Cause you poor—
'cause you different."

He fake-dribble right again.

"Cops drop lives Ferguson-style all over," I say.
"There ain't no place different."

He hold his dribble. I
straighten up.

"What you spinning?" he ask. "That ain't your
think. That someone else."

"I got my own think."

"Yeah . . ." He toss the ball at me. "You do but
that ain't it. That's Catch. That ain't you."

He step off the Court.
Just chill to himself.
Jimmy still holding conference on his phone.

My head junked full with noise.
With the cops asking questions.
With Hilda hot and Money Mike marking me.
Man, I just need relief from all this.

Putting attention to Yo-Yo, seeing how he so
up with fright. I just don't know.
Maybe 'em fools with guns ain't so fooled up
after all.

Man . . . I wish Tony were here.

He'd make clear everything uncool.
He'd sit with me right there courtside.
Share one of 'em Mexican Cokes.
Give me pro then give me con.
Show me how a brother gotta see both sides.
How sometimes 'em sides ain't fair,
but you gotta put attention to 'em.

He'd make it so I could stop the noise and
just . . .

"T," call Jimmy.

"Yeah?"

"Catch been trying you. Say he needs to hold speak."

"He on his way here?"

"Say he can't," Jimmy speak. "Say you gotta meet him
your place."

Nia was gonna be there any sec.
I did not wanna miss time with her.
Especially since she drop word to me
that she wanted to hang.

I throw Jimmy the ball
and
make off the Court.

"Nia be by in a few," I say to Jimmy. "Tell her

to hold time for me. Tell her I didn't mean to
leave her waiting."

"I got you," say Jimmy.

I put eyes on Yo-Yo just as I cut out the fence.
Maybe he right.
Maybe we should all run.

●　●　●

I been waiting on Catch fo' something near an hour.
Where was he?
He wasn't answering his phone.
Not drop a line of word back on text.
I was feelin' the fool in the biggest kind
of way.

Fo' real.

Nia drop message.
Say she meet up with me still
if I really wanna hold the time.
Man, she was the one thing on the right in
all this, and I was sitting there waiting on
Catch, who making me the fool.

I dropped into my sleeveless
hoodie.
Putting eyes to the mirror,
I started thinking on how Nia say I
was an activist.

That brought some power to my look.
I wasn't mad at it.

I halfway into a text to Catch
when he come up the fire escape.
He sweat soaked and rattling loud.
Sounded like he snort half dozen
white lines on a mirror.

"Where you been?" I ask, but he had
no time for my ask.

He was thrust-pumped.
Moving in fast steps.
Moving with potential.

"I done finished it!" he say.

"Finish?" I ask.

"I got tall, man. Oh, T, I got real tall."

He pumped his fists.
He cheering in his own private pep rally.

Then he pulled that piece from the back
of his jeans. That shit make me cautious.
Smoker put my heart out of rhythm.

"What you do, Catch?" I ask. "You ain't
even, man."

"I get shit *right,*" he say. "I dropped him
large."

That I get on the occur.
He done killed Money Mike.
Fo' real.

I put eyes out the window immediate to
see if anyone gather down below yet.

"You shoulda seen his face," he say,
savoring the detail.

I done reached for my phone.
Had to tell the guys.
Had to get him hid.

"I got so fucking tall, T!"

"Catch . . ."

"Yeah?"

"We gotta get you lost," I say. "They gonna
come for you."

He grin.
Damn, was he high on Smoker juice.
I seen brothers who flat-fix someone soar on
that shit like it the needle.

Catch was
f l y i n g !

"Damn, brother, I'm lit on this. I never
felt so moving inside. I walk right up to him
and put the end of this—"

Catch jam the barrel of the heat to his head.

"Catch!"

"*Shhh . . .*" He was so involved. "I'm in memory.
And all I had to do was pull back and

boom!"

He laugh, wild.

"He pissed himself," say Catch. "Can you believe that?
Pissed himself when I shoot him. He feared me!"

He took to pacing.

"I'm goin' down for this," Catch say.
"My sisters—they call the po-lice. Ain't
nuthin' to go back to."

I was mad texting Jimmy.

"You got the guys. Me and Jimmy. Yo-Yo.
We figure how to keep you safe. Get you outta
West Split."

Catch was in think.
Putting pieces into view.

"I gotta finish Money Mike," he say.

"You just flat-fixed him."

"What?" he ask.

Then he laugh.
That big ol' Catch laugh.

"I shoot Pinky, T.

Bam!"

Then it settle.
I didn't know to be relieved
or
more scared. This was edge.
This was edge you can't ease out of.

"You shoulda seen him start," Catch say.
"He pressing how I wasn't man. Pressing
and pushing up on me. And he go for that belt,
and I was like, hell, nah. I ain't your slave. And
I just finish him quiet.

Boom!

He drop back. His chest wet with blood."

My phone lit up.
Jimmy calling.

"Hey," I say to Jimmy. "Yeah, he right here.
How you hear—shit, fo' real?"

I drop attention to Catch. "Jimmy say
the cops all up in your place. That they haul
Pinky out on a stretcher still breathing."

"What?" ask Catch.

"Tiny Lewis pass the word to Jimmy," I say to Catch.
"Jimmy say if you got any cash."

"He still got breath?" Catch ask.

"Come up the side," I say to Jimmy. "Yeah, I
got the window unlocked."

I stopped the phone and went to think.
What a mess, yo.
What a fix to be in.
Had to clear my noise.
I step to pacing,
getting my think in rhythm.

"Catch, listen to me. They'll send you up
good fo' this. You gotta step out."

Catch held his move.
Come right to me.

"You was right, T."

He so sincere in his gesture.
I didn't know what to read on it.

"We shouldn't left that kid there. Ricky-Ricky,
he was soft, man, and brother didn't need to die for
that. He ain't stress no one. Not a day, you know?"

"Catch, you gotta come down—"

"Hear me. You got this so smart, T. Man, I respect that.
I think you punk a lot of the time, but I respect how
you so smart on all this. You always see the angle."

"What angle?" I ask him.

"Right thing angle," say Catch. "That's you. You ain't
fool to get uneven."

"T!" Jimmy shout up the fire escape.

I lean out.
Jimmy tear up the ladder faster than I ever
see him do. Come up the window in mid-speak.

"Street's talking, man," say Jimmy. "We need
to move him quick. Maybe lay him low at the
crackhouse."

That's when the sirens echo-roar.
People below conversating.

Tiny Lewis shout up to me, but I just ignore.

Monica bust in. "T—"

She see us all there.
Catch holding the heat.

"Why we got heat in my brother's room?"
Monica ask.

"No, we good," I say. "Right, Catch?"

Jimmy held time outside the window.

"We got truth down there. It's real," say Jimmy.

Catch chuckle.

"I really wanted to finish Money too," say Catch.
"Go out large. He shouldn't of killed Ricky-Ricky."

Sirens close.
Po-lice had no time to waste.

"Catch, we gotta jet now," I say. "Come up with
a story how you didn't mean to pierce Pinky."

Catch just hold stand.
I didn't know where he was in his think.

"Catch?" I say.

Monica stepped to him.
Put her hand on his arm.
He give her attention.

"They gonna be hard on you," she say.
"You gotta be hard back. Do your time,
but do it well."

"They coming, y'all," say Jimmy.

Catch's high drop.
I seen it real.
He like a boy first day of school,
knowing he can't go home with his mama.

"Try not to go deep in being hard," she say.
"Maybe the law will clear you. Maybe we
see you at our table soon."

Then Catch, he cry.
The hardest brother I know cry.
She put arms 'round him.
"This the only cry you make, you feel me?"

And he just let it out.

Me and Jimmy.
We was long in our look.
Wasn't no escape for Catch.

He going down.
He done.

"You tell your lawyer you've had shit hard,
'cause you did," she say. "Ain't no shame in
tryin' to make it back out here someday. You
got ears?"

"Yeah," he say.

But he was all a wet mess.

"You show your lawyer the scars. And maybe you
do less time inside. Maybe you won't. But
you let that lawyer see. We all know Pinky turn
the volume up in you."

Pigs was beatin' at the door.

"Put the heat down," she say. "Lose your tears.
We gotta face up."

And he done what she say to do.
He take a deep breath and shook off the soft he
just shown all us.

Jimmy and me
followed Monica walking Catch to the front door.

We knew next time we'd see him,
Catch be in court
or
there be hard glass between us.

When the po-lice cuff him, he look at us.

He didn't regret what he done.
He was free.

And that's how Catch went

d o w n .

They Shake Out the Tree to See What Fall

Nia and me been sitting at the park fo'
a while.
Not sayin' much.
Just holding time.
I just didn't know what to say after Catch
get roughed and cuffed.
It was the Fourth, and we'd been up into some
kind of hangin' out, but with Catch in lockup . . .
I dunno.
Felt like everything turned upside and straight
down.

Nia and me was in the shade,
but my skin still sizzling.

My think cooking.
It all just—

"Damn, it's stupid hot," I say, taking stand.
"This heat just gotta end."

"Hey . . ."

I give her attention.

"What's really spinning your think?" she ask.

She put look and effort at me in that way
I know she real, but I just . . . everything so
full of noise.

My ears just ache.

"Ask me a few days ago, and I tell
you I didn't know how I was gonna make it the
summer with Catch leaning on me," I say. "Now I
don't know how I'm gonna make it without
him. I just . . . you ever get so loose in your think?
Where everything feel so uneven?"

"It's a hard thing," she say. "And it's cool if it
is a hard thing, Theodore."

I took to knees.

"We was all—the guys and me, we just wanted to
play hoop, pick up on girls . . ."

She smile on that.
And fo' a sec, so did I.

"We just wanted to be," I say. "It all . . . I
just can't know."

Nia scoot up closer to me. Put
her hand on my chest. Man,
did I just ease fo' a few. Ease
complete.
So much to the moment, I surprised to feel her lips
touched up to mine.

The moment was soft.

When she let loose the kiss, I held steady.
What was she?
She ain't a girl I ever know.

"It's a hard thing," she say. "Not to be up in the rage.
Brothers do it all the time. We both know. You
different, Theodore. When you ain't makin' to
impress with all your big step."

I grin.

"My big step?" I say. "How 'bout you when we have
speak at Nacho's? 'Guess we'll see' when
I ask you be down with a holla?"

"I'm discreet in my choice," she say. "You can't
hate on that."

I just shake out my head.
Smiling.

"But I like holding time with you," she say.

And 'fore I could fix to get something
smooth out, the bass start bouncing.

Gabs come cruisin' up in 'em hot wheels.
Tisha with her like she ain't got no time
to ever spend apart from her.
If Tisha hadn't been sweet on me, I swear
she into Gabs.
I swear!

"Y'all picnic and shit?" say Tisha.

"Why you gotta be like that?" I ask.

"Oh, you got time to hold speak now that you all
up into my cousin."

"Girl, hold your bend," say Gabs, stepping out her car.
"I come down 'cause you need to watch your ass, T."

Gabs intent.

"What's the word?" I ask.

"Money Mike lookin' to smooth some edges. He know
Catch lit up the Wooden Spoon."

"Catch in lockup," I say. "We all cool."

Gabs adjust her stance. Wave her hands in that
Gabs-got-attitude way.

"He struck hot. I'd keep my ass off the streets for a few,"
she say. "I'm just trying to help a brother."

My feel was she wasn't so into helping me as she
found someway to hold speak with Catch.
Her brothers know brothers that work with the cops.
It ain't Mafia or nuthin', but they got connects.

Across the street, kids drop Black Cats, only we didn't
know they was fireworks, and we all drop down
diving like they's bullets.

Soon as Gabs catch on, she was fired up.
She make step right to 'em kids.

"Dumb-ass fool," she say. "I crack your damn heads
if you light up like that again."

They cuss her big.
Real
ON
B I G !

She don't bother.
She get out her phone and snap off a few moments.
Come right back up to us.

"We'll see how they speak when I send over my
brothers," she say.

It was getting dark.
Gabs was gonna roll us all down to the river to
see City fireworks.
Not gonna lie.
I was in no mood fo' hangin' with Gabs or Tisha,
but a li'l time outta the Split
might be a'ight in a day full up on wrong.

Pops and bangs and echoes go ripping the air.

"I'm gonna end them fools," say Gabs.

But 'em sounds.
They was too distinct in their shout.
Those were Smokers.
Someone was firing heat.

Gabs turn over the car. "Every fool in the Split dropping
poppers."

"I ain't on with fireworks," say Tisha.
"They wear my time out."

"Girl, your speak off," say Gabs. "Whose factory
built up in your head?"

Nia put eyes to me.
"What's got you?" she ask.

There it go.
Crackle-pop flooding the air.
"Somebody firing off heat," I say.

Nia and me get immediate.
Put looks outside the car.

"Y'all need to settle your
worry," say Gabs.
She on with the radio,
making the volume hard.

My cell go bright.
Jimmy on the call.

"Soothe that noise," I say to Gabs.

"Hey. We comin' to get y'all—" I say to Jimmy, but
something was off. "What you speak?"

Jimmy was on ramble.
Crying.
I couldn't make him
clear. There was so much
screamin'
and howlin' where he was.

"Where is you?" I say.

And my thoughts—
they all jammed tight.

He said I gotta come.
Say there was a spray down at the Court.
People be flat-fixed.

"Is you shot?" I say.

"Who you on with?" ask Gabs.

"Jimmy, is you shot?" I ask again. "Settle your
think, please, brother. Give me time to hear you
complete."

"Where he dropped?" she ask, and roll the car out
frenzy. "T?"

Jimmy couldn't come clear.
He freakin' like I never heard him.
Not even when his brother got pinched.
Even then, he held his cool.

"Where is he, T?" Gabs ask.

Nia and Tisha kept attention on me.

"The Court," I say to Gabs. "Frenzy this ride."

And she burn every red light.
Scorch the stop signs too.

When we come 'round the corner,
the collection of eyes were all

up on the fence.
The hood
clinging.

Po-lice car lights spray up the walls and street.
Pigs there before us even.
What was so real that make 'em quick?

They was people screamin' and cryin'.
Standin' in the street just occupying.
Phones out
texting
and talking
and snapping pics.

We all jump out the car and run past where
the cops trying to corral us like we a herd.

I dipped
and ducked
and got over to the
fence.

Gabs fight up on some squad car cop
to try and get past, but she held back.

I seen Jimmy.
He covered in blood.

"Jimmy!" I shout.

I rush the Court.

They was bodies.
Bleedin'.

Live.

Dead.

Bleedin'.

They was li'l kids flat-fixed.
Shit, nah.
Hell . . . at least four—five of 'em dropped.

Jimmy come up on me.
His hand trembling.
His cast and shirt wet with blood.

"He killed. He flat-fixed, Theo," say Jimmy,
choked. "He gone."

Jimmy was shakin'.
I never seen him so broken up.
Then I knew.

There.

Flat and fixed.

    Yo-Yo.

He was laid out 'cross the free-throw line.
His thoughts were scattered all over the key.

"We was . . ." Jimmy started. "We was . . .
waiting . . . on Gabs come get us. Couple guys
started up a . . . game. We was just . . . playin'.
Ending the time."

Jimmy put attention to some wounded
brothers. People from the hood trying to
keep 'em revived.

Sirens.
They was immediate.

"You gotta get outta here," Jimmy say. "You gotta run.
Wherever Hilda say. Just go. Tonight, T."

The wind pull on Yo-Yo's T-shirt covered
in blood and sweat and death.
He wanted outta West Split the minute
Pinky brought him here.
Wanted out more than any of us maybe.
He dream it.
All the time.
He seen it, he'd tell me.
Seen how it was gonna be when he was his own man
in his own house
somewhere that ain't
West Split.

He ain't never gonna be none of that.

I couldn't contain.
I was raged.

This ain't how it wrote.
We were—
    we was . . .

"Who done this?" I ask.

Jimmy stunned out, stare off.
Tears burn-rip down his face.

"Jimmy, contain your think, man. Who *done* this?"

His eyes just water.

"He was wild, T," Jimmy say. "His eyes set-out."

"Who?" I say.

"Money Mike. He come in . . . spraying.
Cutting the whole place down."

Yo-Yo.
        Ricky-Ricky.
                And a handful other brothers I ain't know
well enough to remember, but they was
somebody's people.

These li'l kids.
They was all somebody's.

"I just dropped and prayed," Jimmy say. "I just
prayed, man."

Mike and me.
We grow up under the same roof.
Same dinners.
Same stories from Tony and Hilda.
Still he pick up a Smoker to end people's time.

What he done.
It was my cool.
It was my time.

"Let's fix this," I say. "Let's blow up on him
large."

Jimmy didn't ignite.

"I can't," say Jimmy. "I can't do time."

Hot as it was, he was a shiver.

"I can't be finished like Catch," Jimmy say.
"We ain't soldiers, T. We ain't enlisted."

I put eyes on Yo-Yo.

I couldn't see it like Jimmy.

"I gotta roll," I say.

And I made step away from him.

I come out the fence.

Gabs try to hold time. "Is he dead, T?"

But I kept my move past her.
Pushing the fuck up past everyone.
Po-lice.
People.
Get to the outside of all the gather
and
Nia grab up on me.

"I see what you working," she say.

I swing my arm loose.

"You ain't see nuthin'!" I say.

"I see you spinning your think to edge," she say.
"Don't do this."

"Go back to Atlanta," I say. "To your stepdaddy with
money and opportunity. I'm hood. I'm large!"

My legs took speed down the street.

"Theodore, please!" say Nia.

And her voice.
Her smile.
The way she giggle when I clown.
It all fade.

With the turn of a few corners.
With my soul a grease fire.
I coulda lit up the whole city way I felt.
I coulda burnt it all down.

And yeah,
I promised Hilda I wouldn't dig.
I promised Monica I wouldn't dig.
I promised shit I couldn't promise
with Yo-Yo flat-fixed and ended.

More I run, more I know.

I needed to get

h   e   a   t   .

I Was On Fire

Nacho puff on a fat blunt,
washing it back with a 40.
He take time to admire
on his new gold ring. He be flashing
it on the minute I show up
at his place.
It got a bull face up on it with
two diamonds for eyes.
He couldn't keep himself from tellin'
on how he won it on this brother
who lose to the numbers.

"Let me see if I'm on your need," Nacho say.
"You craving heat. No trace."

"I'm in—I need . . ."

I couldn't keep the details level.
My cool was shaky.

"Yeah," I say. "Something I can't be held to. I
know you help Catch and—"

"Catch run big numbers," he say. "He need heat
to honor my payment with some guys. You
don't run fo' me. You got any green?"

I drop my head.
I had six bucks and a quarter in my pocket—
if I lucky.

Nacho puff and drink.

A muscle brother come from upstairs.
I give him attention 'cause he wearing a
piece of big heat. Nacho wave him on back up.

"Nacho, I ain't mean to step and disrespect," I say.
"I just—"

"You hungry, T?" ask Nacho.

I struck off.

"This shit," he say, holding love for the joint. "It's
high-grade, genetically modified smoke. It is
pure and clean and . . . damn. It makes me hungry."

He laugh.
It could shake the ceiling to crumble.

"Makes me crave, you know?" he ask. "Gets me
into the worst kinda eating. Gained five pounds
right across the middle alone."

He grab on his gut fo' confirmation.

"Never on the bud till this," he say. "Now, it's just my
taste. Can't unwant it. You feel me?"

I half-nod, but I didn't feel him complete.

Nacho give sleep to the joint, get up, and
make steps to the kitchen.
I ain't know to hang back or follow,
so I hold steady.

"Come on up in here," Nacho say.

I make step to the kitchen.

"Put hands to the table," he say.

We both strong but his table got weight.
He give snap to a rug and open up the floor.
I give attention in there where he got
all kinds a edge.
He pull out some high heat with a couple
of clips.

"You ever hold heat?" he ask.

I shake my head.

He heavy with his sigh.

"Here's how it go," he say. "Clip . . ."

I half-listening,
half not.
I couldn't keep from thinking on Yo-Yo—
Ricky-Ricky—'em li'l kids.

"T?" say Nacho.

"Yeah . . ." I acknowledge.

"You with this?" he ask. "'Cause if you isn't,
you can still walk it off. We don't need to share
speak on this ever again."

"I ain't got no green," I say.

He nod.

"Consider it a donation to a help-a-brother-in-deep-shit
fund. 'Cause I know you desperate to come to me
and be needing heat. I know I could have advantage
on this and make you owe me. But sometimes we gotta
help a brother to his own advantage. If this is what
you want."

The Smoker in his hand.
That heat was fo' real.
That the kinda shit that change the game.
Hell, it *was* the game.

"I'm on it," I say, holding my hand open.

Nacho give the heat over.
It ain't like no toy gun.
This heat got weight and truth.

"That shit will make you hungry, T," say Nacho.
"It's got a taste."

"I gotta make time," I say.

"See you on the streets," he say.

Just like that,
we was complete.

I extend a shake and make for the front door.

I break fast down the steps.
Sneaks to concrete.
Smoker in the back my shorts.
Heart drumming big bass in my chest.
Ain't no time to chill or second-guess.

And my phone went to popping.
Two missed calls from Nia.

Trejo and Monica both texting me like riot.
Didn't have no time to pace out their
fear.

I was gonna kill my brother.

I had to   r   i   s   e   .

Remember Me Large

I'd been pressing the streets hard.
With the Wooden Spoon ashed,
Jives be scattered. And Money Mike?
He ain't poke his head out the shadow
much less the street light.

But I was gonna find him.
Not sitting still till I do.

I make steps up at Pete's Liquor.
The breeze chill out my sweat
'cause it don't matter that it 10 at night,
I was still baking.

Streets bounced and hummed.
Saturday night. Fourth of July.

People popping fireworks.
Guys smoothing it out with ladies
on street corners.
They didn't have no ember up in their chest.

Few corners down,
I come to the Wooden Spoon.
What left of it.
And
people . . . they gather.
They wasn't mobilizing.
They holding candle with flame.

Up there in the front was Mighty Mildred.
Not on with speak.
Ain't no protest.
They all just stand . . . holding the time.

And I see Smokey up in all that.
His attention cut to me immediate, and
he make effort to step to me intent.

"Your mama got eyes all over for you," say Smokey,
approaching.

I move back up from him.
I ain't got no time fo' his sermon.

"My time is real," I say, making to step down the street.

"How real, Young Black?" he ask.

"Just leave it loose," I say.

"Where you running?" ask Smokey.

I just keep on my go.
Not giving him eyes.

"I got truth to write," I say.

"Now, see, truth and fool is a different thing.
And it look like you writing fool—"

That's when I pulled my Smoker.

"Don't give me names!" I say. "I ain't fool."

He ease, both hands straight to the up.

"I see." He grin. "You got rage now. Is that right?"

"Now?" I say. "Smokey, I been raged."

People hold eyes my way.
They was keeping time with me.

"Nah, Young Black," say Smokey. "You been hope.
You been voice and heart for this community. That's
your truth. That's your story."

He take a step to me.

"See," he say. "You get to write your own ending.
Every moment."

"Don't *peace* me, Smokey," I say. "Don't fill me
up with your easy speak."

He take another step to me.

"Quit on that move," I say. "Hold your step!"

People moving closer.
Mighty Mildred leading their follow.

"You think it easy not to rage violent?" he ask.
"Hardest thing you do as a black man is not rage
violent. That Smoker—that ain't your answer, Young Black.
That is your mistake."

People come to standin' off their stoops too.
Comin' outta their stores.
They lookin' wide.
They witness to me with that heat
pointed at Smokey's chest.

Some 'em people I knew.
Some was just pairs of eyes.

"Don't thug this, T!" say a woman.

"Let's all be cool," say Smokey. "Let's not give
names to this moment. Young Black needs to
speak his uneasy."

"Uneasy? Are you playin?" I ask. "I am rage!"

Three brothers try to rush at me.

"No!" Smokey say to 'em.

I burst hot two shots off in the air.
People drop immediate.
I never popped a shot before—it struck me startled
how a Smoker go.

All of 'em.
They . . . they
FEARED . . .

me?

Mighty Mildred.
She lay on the ground.
I'd put the fear in her too.

All of 'em had made to low but Smokey.
He still standing strong.

"This isn't your war, Young Black," say Smokey.

"He shattered Yo-Yo's thoughts," I say at Smokey.
"They was all over the Court key. They was
everywhere! Soft pieces—he wet with blood.
Li'l kids—they fucking dropped! Flat-fixed."

"I'm sorry for your friend, Young Black," say Smokey.

"I truly am. And for everyone we lose today. We all feeling
the pain tonight. We all have anger and grief, but violence is
not our answer."

Sound of sirens.
Squad car cops not far.
I couldn't hold time with him no more.
It was time to run.

"Young Black, give me eyes," he say. "You got choice —"

"I got no choice."

"Every single moment is choice," he say. "You too
young and life too short for you to settle out with
that kind of nonsense in your hand."

My thoughts jammed quick.
Too many —
 too hard —
too thick.

Yo-Yo — Tony —

Ricky-Ricky.

Too many brothers dropped.
Ain't no escape.
Ain't no gettin' loose.

How could I choose?
Choose to let Money Mike breathe another hour?

He kill two my friends.
He break this hood apart.
Infect it with . . .

And my attention go back to Mighty Mildred.
Her on the ground, fearing me.
I put the scare in her.
She the strongest of 'em all.

I look to Smokey.
His eyes trying to hold church for me.
Trying to get me to ease my fierce.

"I can't let it go," I say. "Somebody gotta finish him."

I start steppin' back from Smokey.

"Young Black, you ain't wrote for bars. You ain't—"

"Peace, Smokey."

I turn and sprint off.
And I mean I was runnin' hard
'cause
I needed the blood rushing my chest.
I needed the extra desperate feeling.
I needed to know I was fierce.

♦ ♦ ♦

I come up on the north end of the Split.
Been keeping my move in the shadows.

Somehow in all it, my side had gone to pulsating pain.
My stitch loose.
But I was too high on rage to loan it time.

I rounded the corner to
Burgers, Rings & More Things.
They run business on the 24.
And how it was that I seen Money Mike waiting fo'
an order, I never can know.
But there he was.
Grinning.
Holding speak on his phone.
Brother behind the bulletproof glass hand off a
greasy white bag to him
and he immediate to chewing on fries.
Carrying on big with his speak and laugh.

I didn't hesitate.
I step large to him.
Gun up direct and pointed at Money.

"You gonna drop me?" ask Money Mike.

"Shut it!" I wave that gun hard. "I'm fierce!"

He didn't laugh.
He didn't even grin.
His face held solid.
He wasn't scared.
And that made me mad!

"I ain't timeless, Mike," I say. "I ain't fool to you."

Jay Ridge come from 'round back.
I drop heat between 'em.
Not knowing which of 'em might pull first.
Jay Ridge hung back.
Didn't reach for his heat.
He just be cool.

"Yo-Yo—Ricky-Ricky," I say. "They had life."

"You want me to cry out for you?" Money Mike say.
"Tell you I'm full of regret for a retard and
a fat boy?"

I hate him.
I hate his eyes.
I hate his stand.
I hate how he come to be so dark inside
even though he always have greed.

I hate.
    I
HATE!

"You was my brother," I say. "We raised up tight.
We play ball. And you jammed all that!"

"T . . ." say Jay Ridge.

I spun the gun to him direct.

"Don't calm me, Jay! I ain't easy. I ain't never gonna
be easy."

"Show me what you is," Money Mike say.
"You ain't timeless? Prove it."

I ram that Smoker right where his heart should
be.
Right where there need to be
conscience,
compassion,
and consideration.

It was hollow.
He was hollow.

That's when it went off.

Not the heat.

me.

Everything come to moment.
Who is you?
That's what Catch ask me that day outside DJ Spin's.
Who is me?

Theodore Todd Clark, I answer in my head.
I never enlist.
I never want to drop a soul on the real.
I never carry heat.

But I had heat in my hand.

Tears.

They stream.
And I was madder than
hell and thunder and all the war
the world ever seen
'cause I wasn't wanting or needing 'em.

But there they make.
'Em tears just bubble right up and slide on down.
I put eyes on that Smoker.
I wasn't that heat.
I wasn't that bullet ready to end my brother.
This wasn't being fierce. This was fool.
It wouldn't bring none of 'em back who was
gone.

I drop the heat to my side.

"Are you for real?" ask Money Mike. "You step
to me like you got a set. What a fucking waste you is.
I can't do you no more favors. I'd be marked up
and down. And life too short to end 'cause you grow
a conscience for some stupid retard, too fool to come
out the rain."

"He didn't come out of the rain," I say. "Because he like
how it feel on his skin."

Sirens.
Someone call the po-lice.
They was coming hard.

The speed of all the next.

It's so fast—so slow.
How can it be both?
Dunno.

The first shot . . . that's real.
I'd never been hit.
It stun and shake and all the adrenaline
sprint-rush
direct to that hole in my gut.
I drop back hard.

The second shot.

It easier 'cause it's quick I guess.
'Cause I was distracted by the hurt
from the first.

It's hard to express.

It so fast—so slow.
How can it be both?

I let go.

My eyes shut.
I couldn't watch what was real.
Money Mike was intent to make
me cold forever.

The pain so rich
and honest

and the breeze
  done what it could to cool me off.

And I was wet with sweat and blood.
Quick—
went to memory of Hilda and Tony.
They making dinner.
Friday-night spaghetti.
Monica homeworking fo' school.
Mike 'fore he Money playing card tricks
on me.

He could make a thing disappear.

I see Nia giggling and Jimmy with Gabs.
I rush every picture I could make on
to not see death stepping to me in big black boots
that could make the earth spin to fade.

I'm scared, I say to Hilda in my think.
And I swear, I just wanted her to hug up on me
like when I was li'l.
Squeeze me till I could hardly hold still.

Dying.
It make you feel the world of every moment special
on the immediate.
Every
        thing
                was
                        immediate.

This—

would be how it all be wrote.

On the hot street.
In the dark.
Sirens closer but not close enough.

Breathe.
Smokey would say. Breathe, Young Black.

But my breath struggle.
Money Mike ready.
He point that heat.
He had so much potential right then—

Hilda, Tony, Nia, the Guys,
Ricky-Ricky, Mildred, Smokey, Old Man Charlie,
the Wooden Spoon,
Pinky, Tisha, Gabs, Monica, the hood, the hood, the hood,
the hood, the . . .

B R E A T H E

The third shot—

C R A C K E D !

Money Mike drop, flat-fixed,
on the sidewalk.

Hole

clear through his split open head.
His eyes flicker to cold.

"T," say Jay Ridge.

Mike's eyes was cold.
He flat-fixed forever.
He wasn't standing up ever.
His knuckles were bruised.
Nails dirty.
His whole body seem
    smaller.

"You got ears?" ask Jay Ridge.

Jay Ridge took knees beside me.
He'd capped my brother.

"You ain't finished," he say. "Not you."

Not you?

And
  there
      I go.

I click to memory of 'em Jives holding up the li'l grocery.
Tony dropped and that one Jive with the Smoker gonna
finish me but . . .
    Not him, the other guy say.

"You spare me?" I say. "At the store."

"I'm sorry for Tony," say Jay Ridge, his voice crumble.
"He done me good. Always. Just like you."

He press on my gut.
I howl.

"Shit!" I say.

"Put your hand to this," he say.

Po-lice red and blue light splatter
on the wall—on Jay Ridge's face.

He lean into me, "Big Joe says this makes y'all even."

"Get your hands up!" shout a cop.

The street.
The everything was gettin' faded.
Jay turned to the po-lice.
My heat in his hand.

"I got heat!" Jay Ridge held his hands up.

At least, I think he did.
They seem up.

"Drop your fucking weapon!"

I don't see what happen direct.
It was all so bright from the squad lights.
Jay Ridge was a fuzzy kinda outlined shape.

> "Put your face to the ground!" shout the cop.
> "Now!"

Cops charge Jay Ridge direct.
They rough him tough
it seem.

"Never look back, T," Jay Ridge say.

Po-lice didn't rough me.
They ask if I could hold speak.
They ask who I is.
I was trembling too intent in my skin.
So hot—
         so cold.
The breeze did what it could.
More sirens.
I had to be cool.
Relax.
Look up. Way up.
Like Tony would from the stoop.

In the City, you can't see the stars.
So you just gotta make 'em up.
Imagine where they might shine.
Imagine where they might fall.
Then you wish.

I made a lot of wishes laying there,
bleeding on the sidewalk.

Even when the ambulance peeps come,
I just keep looking
up
and
wishin'.

Past the streetlights.
Past building tops.
Past the clouds.
I was makin' all the wishes
I could 'fore they was ended.

'Fore I

d e a d .

When We Was Fierce

I was touch.
I was go.
That's what Monica say to me
when I really come to
  in the hospital.

I'd been on the sleep for a few days
almost straight.
It was all a dream.

When I come alert on the real,
Monica cry something big.
Bigger than her belly swoll.

Hilda ain't make no scene when she

first come to hold time. She ain't let out rage
or hot air or nuthin'.

Don't think that didn't strike me curious,
but it just how she was.
She hold my hand snug like she never have
plans to let go and make big speak with Tony
at the ceiling.

Thanking him fo' holding me safe.

Me and Hilda, we able to hear each other speak
during those days. Not always.
I mean, Hilda hard to bend to a thought.
But she try.

Trejo come hold time with me.
He the first to give me the know about
what went down with Jay Ridge and the po-lice.
Trejo say Jay Ridge confess to flat-fixing Money Mike.
Say how Money tried to drop me just out of spite
fo' not enlisting.
Jay Ridge tell 'em Money stomp out Ricky-Ricky.
And he didn't roll nuthin' 'bout me
showing with that Smoker.
No one in the hood said a thing 'bout seeing me
with one neither. It all just kinda went away.

That was a lucky I know I never gonna score twice.
Not that I intend to need it.

Trejo give me truth on how it shatter him

to hold think on me almost ended.
His eyes even held some water when he say it.
I knew that truth wouldn't keep him from
staying in the Skins, but I hold out hope
he leave all that someday.
Maybe we could play Mexican street ball like
we done when we was kids.
It's off the level I know, but thoughts just come
at you when you got time to just lay up.

Those days in the hospital were long. Stretched
out just till the heat wave broke. Rain come
down like Noah was building an ark.
I swear it was on the try to wash away all the blood
and tears
and sweat from the streets.

Nuthin' change in the hood as far as slingin'
and money-making on the sly.

Nacho and the Skins turn numbers deep.
Another brother rise up to hold obedience to the Jives.

But no one come near me.
No one had any cause.

We was done with all that.

The summer come and run quick.
Nia and me kick message some of the time
after she leave back for Atlanta.
She dating this guy, and she on like with him solid,

so we friends.
Ain't never had a girl who just a friend.
We see how that all spell out.

Hilda still working two jobs,
talking about needing three.
Monica bring that baby up into this world
And give it over a few days later. We don't
talk about it much.
I know being back in school is where she on,
but I think it hard . . . letting that baby loose.
I mean, I can't really know.

We was days deep into October when Hilda
make through the door big.
She's just got that way, you know?

Her and Monica laugh.
Run thought at each other.
It caught me good . . . made me easy.
Couldn't hold memory the last time
they laugh together.

"Theodore?" Hilda call out.

"Yeah?" I call back from my room.

"Don't 'yeah' and get in here," she say.

I was home working down that math they
give me. Didn't need interruptions. But

Hilda was intent.
And I still ain't never wanna mess with
Hilda being intent.

She was dealing out mail on the kitchen
table. There was a letter.

ELM COUNTY JUVENILE CORRECTIONAL FACILITY

was up in the corner.
Catch had written me back.

"Should I be uneasy?" Hilda ask.

Monica didn't look up from her mail pieces.
"He good," she say. "Right, Theo?"

"Yeah," I say to Monica. "It's all on the up, Hilda."

Just like that, Hilda let it sit.

I stepped back into my room and climbed out
on the fire escape.
The bump-thump of bass boom music
split the street noise as I settle in.

I hesitated on reading Catch's letter.
It had been a month and some days since I wrote him.
Told him in my own speak how everything
shook out on the streets. How I was sorry
I couldn't kill Money Mike for Yo-Yo and Ricky-Ricky.

How he was wrong to shoot Pinky but right too.
And how I didn't know how one action could be both,
but was glad he didn't end Pinky.

I tore open Catch's letter.
Unfolded it and chuckle at a drawing of the four
us guys. He always had a way to spin cartoons of us.

> *I'm not gonna lie.*
> *Lemme tell you, T.*
> *It's hard up in here.*
> *Seen some fucking tough-ass brothers*
> *break. You can't imagine how they do in*
> *here.*
>
> *Means the world to get your words few weeks*
> *back, T.*
> *Took me some time to think on it. I've had a*
> *lot of fire*
> *burning my chest. Got tossed into seclusion, and*
> *that shit will earn you time to think . . . hard!*
>
> *My moms ain't been by since the judge drop*
> *sentence on me. I ain't bothered.*
> *She too far gone to know me no more.*
> *Sometimes I think that's just how shit goes.*
>
> *Your sister sent me some cookies she bake.*
> *They wasn't half-bad. Wasn't half-good either.*
> *Bet you're laughing right on that, T.*
>
> *Didn't matter how they taste. It was the effort*

she make that count. She send me some books
too. One by this Mexican out in LA, California
who useta gang bang monster hard and got out.
'Nother 'bout this brother grow up in a hood
like ours, and he figure a way out.
Then she sent me a book on G.E.D. Maybe
I get on that last one first. Maybe you was right.
Maybe education help a brother.

Spend a lot of time practicing my spit. Don't
think I'll get some record deal, but it passes the
clock. Lift a lotta weights. Every night before they
call lights, I push up a hundred and two in the bunk
room. It tires me, so I don't hear some guy crying
in his pillow. Man, some guys really go to wailing.
Be honest, I can't fault it.

There always someone wanna make you their
slave or master in here. Thought about what
you said. Why can't we be level?
Why someone always gotta bow down?

The world fucked up, T.
Not sure how exact to get it better.
But I'm taking time to think on it. Even outside
Isolation.

I'm always gonna be a black man with a sheet.
Maybe, I dunno . . . there's some way to rise above.
That would be something, huh, man?
To rise? Outta all this? That would be large, bro.
Real large.

Hey, I gotta finish this out.
Keep your head tight. Don't cave to nobody
but Hilda. Maybe your sister.
Damn, your sister fine.
Shit!
Serious, man. Stay straight. You and Jimmy.
And I ain't got hate on you for not drawing heat
on Money Mike.
It ain't never been your way, so I'm glad you
stayed to the angle.

See y'all soon, I hope. Peace!
Catch

I folded his letter back up in the envelope
and jam it in my back pocket.

Looking out at the hood from the fire escape,
it all seemed small. Smaller than I ever
remember. Useta be the whole world on
the brick upright and cracked concrete.

Dunno. Just all looked different right then.

Started thinking. My brain so full of think.

When the summer started, me and the guys had
all these ideas. How we'd feel up some girls,
drink Mexican Cokes, and shoot hoop.
Catch would win that spit contest and net
some big rap deal.
Yo-Yo wanted to go big and break the world record

for tricks with that bullet-red Duncan.
Him tagging with spray that was outta sight.
And Jimmy . . . he just wanted to keep us all
cool. No heat. No hurt.
Alive.

Jimmy left West Split just 'fore school start
up.
Didn't text or call. I just wait on him at the Court
one day, and he never show.
Ask his mom what's down.
She say he gone to California to live with his
brother.
Gone to some li'l town I never heard of till I
look it up. Place got sand instead of snow.
Ocean instead of City Pool.
More I thought on it, more I made it my cool that
he had to cut out the way he did.
Sometimes a brother need to keep face.
'specially after so many tears.

Not sure what all happen from here on.

Sometimes it squeeze and hold on me . . .
everything that went down.
I get sick to my stomach.
Feel like I can't keep my breath.

Monica talk me through.
Remind me I'm still here.
But it's hard without the guys.
Without Ricky-Ricky.

Monica say loss will stay with you forever.
Hilda says it hurts a little less by time.
Smokey. He tell me just to take one day.
Then another day.
When it all ready to settle clear, it will.

We was fierce when we all was rolling down
the street that day Ricky-Ricky got dropped.
But then
  everything changed.
A good kid got flat-fixed and wasn't no
reason for it that wasn't fool.
No reason at all.

Too many brothers dying.
Too many brothers locked up.
Too many brothers forgetting how to dream.

Will I be one of 'em?

It's like Jimmy say in the alley that day about
me not being finished.

I ain't finished.
I'm here.
No Smoker.
Trying to make it clean and clear out.

We'll see how it all go.

Acknowledgments

I'm a fortunate witness to a creative revolution. It is a revolution fought with language. From the thin blue lines of notebook paper to the back of wadded-up receipts. From text messages to thought bubbles in graphic novel panes. It is the raw and real, clipped and refined—it is the moment where young people reclaim their voice.

This book is part of that creative revolution, I hope. Thank you to my editor, Joan Powers, who trusted me to take this story to its edges. Thanks to my agent, Erin Murphy, who empowers me to take risks that matter. Thanks to rock-star editorial assistant Allison Cole, who insured this novel open with Tupac and diligently worked with me on copyediting nuances at the final hours before print. My friends: Margaret Coble, Galen T. McGriff, Pat Zietlow

Miller, Frances Gordon, Karl Miller, Sally Derby, Audrey Patrick, Dave & Tanya Bartlett, and *mi hermana* from another mama, Amy, thank you.

Thanks to those who inspire me: Yuyi Morales, Jason Reynolds, Andrea Cascardi, Kwame Alexander, Kathy Erskine, G. Neri, J. Don Luna, and Vincent J. Cardinal.

Special shout-out to educators Kim Summers, Cassie Cox, Carlos Ulloa, Ana Rodriguez, and Erica Scott and librarians Brenda Kahn, Melody Ann, and Cynthia Hurd. I never met you, Mrs. Hurd, but your dedication to people will carry on.

As always, infinite love for my brother Kurt; his wife, Anouck; and Esperanza & Ayden.

Most important . . .
For Joe Prather, Kamari, Kerwin, Ana, and all the voices that are
    fighting to be heard.
For the kids I've walked the streets with
and shared time with in alternative high schools,
homeless shelters, after-school programs,
and juvenile detention centers.
Your future has not been written.
May you always be fierce.
This is your moment.
Pick up a pen or a pencil or a crayon—take your story to the page.
Let them know you have a voice.
Let them know you will never be counted out!